"What's going on," she asked.

"Nothing," Casper said, but his eyes were dark.

"Don't lie to me. What's wrong?"

He glanced over at her and took off his cowboy hat, then set it on the dashboard. He ran his hands over his face and through his hair in exasperation. "I just think it's going to be better if you get away from all this—this investigation."

"What happened?" she asked, trying to stop the hurt from leaking out into her voice.

All she had been trying to do for the past two days was solve this so they both could get their jobs done. Now, after a strange meeting with the Canadian Mounties, she was on the outs. It didn't make sense.

"You didn't do anything, Lex. I promise."

She tried to remind herself they were only friends, and maybe barely that. Sure, they had shared the kiss in the woods, but ever since they had gotten caught he had barely been able to look at her.

"Is this because of what happened...you know, back there?" She motioned in the direction they'd come from.

But she was sure he knew *exactly* what she was talking about.

WILD MONTANA

DANICA WINTERS

HARLEQUIN INTRIGUE®

To Lane—

You work miracles.

Acknowledgments

This book wouldn't have been possible without the help of my fans. Thank you for taking a moment out of your lives to leave a review, come to book signings and send me notes, cookies and even the occasional bottle of vodka. You inspire me to keep writing when the going gets tough. Thank you.

ISBN-13: 978-1-335-72082-5

Wild Montana

Copyright © 2017 by Danica Winters

Recycling programs for this product may not exist in your area.

www.Harlequin.com

Printed in U.S.A.

Danica Winters is a multiple award-winning, bestselling author who writes books that grip readers with their ability to drive emotion through suspense and occasionally a touch of magic. When she's not working, she can be found in the wilds of Montana, testing her patience while she tries to hone her skills at various crafts—quilting, pottery and painting are not her areas of expertise. She believes the cup is neither half-full nor half-empty, but it better be filled with wine. Visit her website at danicawinters.net.

Books by Danica Winters

Harlequin Intrigue

Smoke and Ashes
Dust Up with the Detective
Wild Montana

CAST OF CHARACTERS

Agent Casper Lawrence—A sexy former FBI agent with a checkered past who now works for the Customs and Border Protection Agency. Brother of Robert and Jeremy Lawrence, but thanks to his demons, he keeps his distance from his family.

Ranger Alexis Finch—A beautiful, strong and independent woman. She lives her truth whether or not it makes those around her happy, even when it comes to playing by the unwritten rules at her job as a park ranger at Glacier National Park.

Travis Yellowfeather—Alexis's ex-husband, a fellow ranger at Glacier National Park and a man who has a closet full of skeletons.

Denver Dragger—Alexis's boss and the head park ranger. He wants Alexis to focus on the park's need to get ready for the winter. She plays along, but hates the fact he is pulling her off the case and takes matters into her own hands—putting her beloved job on the line.

Evan Steel—Handsome deputy for the US Marshals, who has extensive experience investigating motorcycle gangs.

Razor—Right-hand man for the president of the Hells Keepers motorcycle club.

Lois Trainer—Razor's girlfriend in Columbia Falls, a small town that borders Glacier Park and its unmanned back entrance—the perfect place to gain access to the park without being noticed. She is also implicated in a large drug-distribution ring.

Peter Kagger—The secretary for the Alberta chapter of the Hells Keepers, who isn't afraid to leverage everything he has to get what he wants.

Prologue

Seven. Most people thought the number was lucky. *He'd* even thought it had been lucky. This was supposed to be his seventh trip, the last run of the season, the last cleanup before he could head to Mexico and lie on the beach for the winter. Señoritas, sunshine, cervezas…everything he needed to be happy.

Yet now as he stared down the predator, he could have sworn seven was a curse.

The grizzly hopped on its front legs like a dog ready to play, but from what little he knew about bears, it wasn't an action that meant fun and games…no, that was an action that meant danger.

He eased back a step as he held the bear's gaze. Its beady black eyes bore into him, sizing him up.

Not for the first time in his life, he wished he were eight feet tall.

"Good bear," he said, putting his hands up. "Good bear." He turned to look over his shoulder, but the man he'd been sent there to meet was gone. "Damn him."

Without warning, the bear charged. The fur on its shoulders rippled, its gold tips harsh against the white snow. He screamed, the sound echoing through the high mountain valley.

The beast didn't slow down.

He turned to run, but it was too late. The griz hit him like no force he had ever experienced. Its putrid, hot breath seared the back of his neck as he fell to the ground. Heat and pain spread through his body as the predator's teeth met bone.

He closed his eyes, pain burning through him as the gunshot rang out.

The world, the pain, the fear—everything stopped.

Chapter One

Alexis Finch forced her body up the steep trail and toward the location the hikers had described. Ravens swooped through the air above her, calling out secrets to their comrades as they flew west. Even though she hiked nearly every day through the backcountry of Glacier National Park, each step was torturous. The altitude made her breath come faster, but she focused her attention on the thick pines that surrounded them, and she ignored the pain that shot up from her tired calves.

"Ranger Finch," the Customs and Border Protection agent called from behind her.

She was thankful as she stopped and turned back, taking the moment to catch her breath and shift the straps of her backpack, as they had started to cut into her shoulders. "Hmm?"

Casper Lawrence stopped beside her, his cheeks pink and a sheen of sweat covering his tanned face. She found comfort in the fact that after more than three miles of this uphill battle, the handsome agent was hurting just as badly as she was. "According to the GPS, this should be the spot." He motioned around them.

The hillside was covered with thick, frost-bitten grasses, timber and patches of snow that hid in the shadows. No evidence of a struggle. No blood. No fresh tracks.

"Look," she said, pointing toward the ravens overhead. "No matter what the GPS says, we follow the birds. Listen to nature. It'll give us all the information we need." She cringed as she realized how much she sounded like a bumper sticker, but as she spoke the words she knew they were true, especially when it came to finding a body.

If she'd learned anything in working as a law enforcement park ranger in the park for the last five years, it was that the only thing she could trust was Mother Nature's fickle attitude. She did as she pleased, and danger could be found in the moments that a person underestimated her power. It was easy to identify the people who had misjudged her; they were usually the ones Alexis and the other rangers were sent into the backcountry to find—or the ones whose bodies they were sent in to recover.

"I like nature, but don't you get tired of being

stuck out here?" Casper looked up, taking off his Stetson and wiping away the thin line of sweat that it had collected. His slightly-too-long chestnut hair hung down over his caramel-colored eyes, obviously blinding him from the beauty that surrounded them.

He gazed toward the birds and slipped the hat back on his head.

"Stuck? Out here?" She laughed. It was hard to imagine being stuck in a place like this, where there was only open sky and rugged earth. "I'd much rather be out here than in some tiny apartment. I had enough of that kind of thing in college." She glanced over at Casper and his tan-colored hat. The wide brim cast his face in shadows, accentuating his firm, masculine jaw.

"Your girlfriend give you that?" she asked, motioning toward his hat.

He looked at her like he was trying to get a read on her. "I bought it in Kalispell a few years back." He took it off again, spinning the brim of it in his hands like he was talking about an old friend.

"Cowboy hats are a lost art," she said as she started to move up the trail.

A lot could be learned about a man by the hat he wore, whether he was a rancher or a weekend cowboy. Each style meant something different, but from the dents, the line of the crown and the sweat marks, it was clear he wanted to look like a cattleman.

"You grow up on a ranch?" she asked, excited that maybe they had some common footing.

He gave her that look again, like he just couldn't make heads or tails of her, but rather than making her feel uncomfortable, she liked the feeling of keeping him guessing. Maybe she spent too much time alone, but being an enigma to this too-handsome cowboy made heat rise from her core.

"No, my family comes from Butte."

"Ah," she said, forcing herself to look away from the agent. "A Butte boy... So you're Irish?"

He sent her a sexy half grin that made her nearly trip over her own feet. "Yep."

"You visit a lot?"

"Last time I was there was for my brother's funeral," he said, his tone hard.

"I'm so sorry."

Casper shrugged. "Robert had a lot of problems."

From his tone she could tell he didn't want to talk about it, so she dropped it and let the sounds of their footfalls fill the space between them. It made sense that he, the man who seemed to constantly be looking at her as if he was digging for something, came from a family of secrets in the rough and tumble mining town.

They crested the hill that led to Kootenai Lake. The crystal-clear water mirrored the snowcapped, jagged outcrops of Citadel Peak; it was an almost perfect picture, like one of the many postcards they sold at their visitor center. A raven cawed, pulling her attention away from the breathtaking view.

The bird sat in an old snag and picked at a bit of meat that it held in its grip.

"I think we're in the right place," she said, motioning toward the feasting bird. "Where did the hikers say they spotted the body?"

"When they stopped at the border crossing to report their findings, they said there wasn't much of a body to speak of. All they said they found was a boot. Apparently, they marked the area." As he spoke, an icy breeze blew off the lake. Near the west bank a piece of pink plastic duct tape fluttered on the bough of a tree, catching his attention. "There," he said, pointing in its direction.

She hurried over to the tape, the weariness she had been feeling suddenly dispelled by a surge of adrenaline.

Hopefully the hikers had been wrong. Hopefully this was nothing more than some tourist's castoff and not what they had assumed. If it was, she and Casper would have a mess on their hands and that, at the end of the main season, was the last thing that either one of them needed.

She pinched the tape as if it would give her the answers she needed, yet the plastic remained silent.

There was nothing at the base of the tree except needles and pinecones. No doubt that since the hikers had left this morning, the birds and other scavengers had been at work.

Alexis dropped the heavy pack she'd been carrying and started searching the ground around the pine. The grass had been mashed, and there was a faint trail of broken stems that led into the forest. She followed the game trail away from the lake and deeper into the timber.

"Ranger Finch?" Agent Lawrence called out, with a hint of panic in his voice.

She looked up from the nearly invisible game trail and turned. Agent Lawrence was nowhere in sight. "Yep," she called. "I'm over here."

There was the sound of breaking twigs and his cussing as he bulled through the timber. He may have been an agent, but he was clearly no ninja. He broke through the grips of the trees and came into view. There was a scratch across his cheek, complete with a speckle of blood.

"Don't run off. I don't need two bodies to recover."

She chuckled. Based on his trail-breaking skills, she was more likely to make it out of the underbrush long before he would.

"Don't worry, city boy, I won't leave you again if you're scared," she teased.

He wiped at his cheek. "All right, I had that coming, but seriously…"

She waved him off as she started moving. "Got it, Agent Lawrence."

"And quit calling me Agent. Only tourists call me that. I'd like to think that since you let me tag along on this one, we're at least kind of friends."

Kind of friends… She smiled at the thought.

In truth, she had been glad when he'd called and, due to the proximity to the International Border, they had decided to work this case together. For the first time since she had started working here, she had been looking forward to the end of the main season so she could find a little more distance from the tension between her and her ex. Until then, this cowboy and their kinda friendship could be her perfect distraction.

There was a scurry of movement as a small brown animal sprinted through the underbrush. Her body tensed as she stopped and tried to see the animal, but it had disappeared through a line of bushes. It could have been a pine marten or any number of other small mammals, but the unexpected movement made her even more wary than she had been before.

There had to be a body around here somewhere

if the smaller animals were scavenging. No doubt bears, mountain lions and wolves were in the area. The scent of death would have brought every hungry mouth from miles around. She turned to warn Casper but stopped. He had a gun in his hand; it was half-raised.

"Little jumpy, eh? You can put the gun away, Casper," she said. "If that had been a bear, it wouldn't have done you much good anyway."

"Hey now, I'm a good shot," he said, sheepishly dropping the gun back into its holster.

"I doubt that," she said, thinking back to the days she had spent plinking cans off the tops of fence rails at her family's ranch. Back at home in the Bitterroot Valley, everyone knew her family— and her history. It was nice to meet someone who couldn't judge her for her faults.

She moved toward the brush where the animal had first appeared. There, tucked under the branches, was a man's REI hiking boot. Its sole was worn where the ball of the foot would have been.

"I got it," she called.

Casper stepped carefully, avoiding the dried twigs that littered the ground in what she had to assume was his attempt to be quiet. He stopped beside her. "What is it?"

"See for yourself." She lifted the branch so he could see the man's boot.

"Do you think someone just left it behind?" he asked. "Maybe it dropped out of their pack or something."

"No one just leaves behind their hiking boots, not here. Not when they still have a few miles to get back to the nearest trailhead."

She took a few pictures to document the scene and then gingerly pulled the shoe out by its well-worn laces. The boot's leather had dark brown stains over the toe and around the ankle to the heel. She flipped it up.

Her breath hitched in her throat.

Inside the shoe was the mucky white color of bone and dried dark red strings of chewed tendons and eviscerated flesh.

Whoever had put this shoe on was still wearing it.

She let go of the laces and stepped back from the gruesome object. She'd seen plenty of dead bodies, but nothing quite like this. It was so deformed and mutilated that, if it hadn't been in a shoe, she almost wouldn't have believed it had once belonged to a person.

"What do you think happened to this guy?" she whispered, out of some instinctual response to being around the dead.

"I have no idea," Casper said, shaking his head. "But we have a place to start finding out."

"How's that?" she asked, looking up at him.

"We know the guy didn't hike out." Casper ran his hand over the stubble that riddled his jaw. "Now we just have to find the rest of his body."

Chapter Two

The Flathead Emergency Aviation Resources, or FEAR, helicopter touched down near the lake, its blades chopping at the air and making white caps on the crystal-blue water. Casper always hated this moment, the instant when the chain of command shifted and their team lost some of its control. Most times, he could find his best evidence and the most answers before a mess of officers showed up. Yet this time, he had to admit it was different. This was a death in which the only witnesses were the animals who had feasted on the remains and the two wayward hikers who had found the body. With an incident like this, they needed extra hands on deck—no matter how badly he wished it could just be him…and Alexis Finch.

It had been nice following her up that trail, her tight green pants stretching over hips and her full, round curves. It had made the brutal hike a little more bearable—and he'd found a new love for standard-issue forest service pants.

Alexis stood beside him, lifting her hand to shield her eyes from the dust the chopper's blades kicked up. She squinted as she glanced over at him. "Let the party start," she said with a cynical smile that made his gut clench.

He forced himself to look away from her full lips and the way the fine lines collected around the corners of her eyes when she glanced over at him.

He had to focus on their case.

It was only out of sheer luck that the hikers had come to him and he'd convinced his boss that he was vital to the investigation. His boss had only let him go when he'd lied and told him that there was some evidence that the hiker may have crossed the border—which landed the case squarely in their lap. If they screwed this investigation up his boss had, in no uncertain terms, told him he would be out.

This was his last chance.

His next stop on the career line was a desk job at a DMV somewhere—if he was lucky. Then again, he'd already been sent to the Siberia of the contiguous United States: a tiny stand-alone border crossing station on the side of a lake only accessible by ferry or foot. It was the CBP's equivalent of exile.

Things couldn't get much worse.

The coroner bent down out of the rudder wash and hurried toward them. The man was pale, but when he straightened up as he neared them, Casper noticed the telltale spider veins and reddened nose of a major alcoholic.

"Where're the remains?" the man yelled above the sound of the slowing motor.

Alexis motioned for him to follow her.

As they drew near, Casper stared at the blood-covered leather boot. It was strange, but it looked exactly like one he had bought at REI earlier that summer. He wondered if somewhere along the way the man who'd worn this one had stood beside him in the store, passing the boot from one hand to the other as he decided if it was really the right one for him—just as Casper had done.

He pushed the thought from his mind. He had to remain detached.

It was the moment when things became real that emotions came into play, and emotions had been what had gotten him into trouble with the FBI. They had wanted the Robo-Cop—the man who could run through the blood and muck and then stand there and eat a sandwich without thinking about the residue of life that stained his footprints and constantly filled his reality.

If only he was better at disconnecting his head

from his heart—life and work would be so much easier.

"Nothing else?" the coroner asked, like he appreciated the fact that there was so little to transport back to the medical examiner.

Alexis shook her head. "No. As of this time, these are the only remains we've managed to locate."

"We need to get a full canvass on the area." The coroner stepped out of the timber and motioned toward the helicopter.

Two rangers stepped out of the chopper and rushed toward them. From the puckered look on Alexis's face she must have known the men. She gave a begrudging grunt as the guys made their way over and stopped next to them. The dark-haired ranger kept looking over at her like he was trying to get her attention, but she gave him the cold shoulder.

"Where do you want us to start, Hal?" the dark-haired ranger asked.

Alexis turned to the man. "I have a place you can go, Travis—"

"Travis, you take the northern trail," the coroner interrupted, giving them both a disapproving glance. He turned to the other ranger, a blond. "John, you take the south. We only have a couple of hours before nightfall. The pilot needs us out before he's flying in the dark. Make it count."

Though he couldn't say the same of the two rangers, he liked the coroner. He'd always appreciated the type of people who cut the small talk—all business and no bull. Life would be so much easier if everything worked that way; no politics, no favorites, no strings.

"Alexis, you go east and Agent—"

"Lawrence," Casper answered.

"Agent Lawrence, you go west," Hal said, motioning to each of them in the respective directions. He pointed to his radio clipped to his waist. "If any of you find something, I'm on four." He turned away and went to work, going over Alexis's pictures and her notes about the scene and its presentation.

Travis and John moved away through the timber.

Casper started to move west. He didn't make it far before Alexis grabbed his arm and pulled him to a stop. "Let's work together."

Her face was neutral, but he couldn't help getting the feeling that she was frightened.

He looked in the direction of the coroner, but the man was busy with his work and didn't seem to notice the break in his ranks. "Hal doesn't seem like the type who likes rule breakers." He nudged his chin in the man's direction.

"First of all, this is my investigation. He had no business taking control of how I'm running this scene," Alexis said, her voice flecked with anger. "Besides, he'll be happy if we find something, and there's a better chance to find something if we actually work together in canvassing the area."

"You're the boss," Casper said, but in truth he was more than happy to be working with her. He liked being alone—he'd grown accustomed to it over the last year of working at the border crossing—but she made the constant hum inside him grow still and calm.

They walked a few arm lengths apart, moving through the timber and skirting around the lake. Every time she crawled over a bit of deadfall she would sigh, and after what must have been the hundredth tree he was certain that soft moan would be ingrained in his memory forever.

She sighed again and his thoughts moved toward the other moments she would make that noise… How her body moved… How she would look without those green pants and that khaki shirt. Maybe she was the kind of woman who liked lingerie, or maybe not. A girl like her was probably more of the comfort type, real.

She glanced over her shoulder as she was stepping over a downed log, and the leg of her pants caught on a sharp branch. She stumbled, her body moved slowly through the air as she tried to pull her leg from the gnarled grip of the broken bit of deadfall. Yet as she struggled, she lost her balance.

He rushed to her side. "Are you okay?"

He released her pant leg from the stabbing bit of wood. It had torn through her pants, making an L-shaped hole.

"I'm fine," she said, trying to move but her body was wedged between two logs.

"I thought you were the expert in the woods, Ms. Ranger," he teased, trying in vain to make the embarrassed look on her face disappear. He held out his hand, waiting for her to take his peace offering.

She stared at his hand for a second. "Even experts make mistakes." She struggled to push herself up.

He reached down and took her hand, not waiting for the beautiful, stubborn woman to accept his help.

There was a surge of energy between them and her eyes grew wide, her mouth dropping open almost as if she felt it, as well. He pulled her to her feet and quickly let her go. She was gorgeous standing there, her mouth slightly agape as she flexed her fingers.

"Thanks for the hand. I guess it's been a long day." She glanced in the direction they'd come, almost as if she was expecting to catch a glimpse of someone. "I'm off my game."

"Don't worry, I got your back." He felt stupid as the words left his mouth. He wanted to say so much more, ask her so much more. Yet it wasn't the time or the place. The spark he'd felt was probably nothing more than residual adrenaline leftover from their hike, or some misplaced stress from their findings.

She opened her mouth to say something, stopped, and turned away. He moved ahead of her, taking the lead so he could help her through the deadfall. This time her movements were slow, deliberate.

He stopped when he spotted a patch of animal hair on the trail in front of him. It looked like fresh fur, its golden tips still sparkling in the little bit of sunshine that managed to break through the trees. "I think we got something here."

She moved closer. "Look at those tracks," she said, pointing toward the gouges in the earth beside the tuft of fur. The holes were deep and massive, and they littered the ground in the shape of a nearly perfect circle. "There must have been some kind of fight." Bending down, she picked up a piece of the dirt and inspected it, like she could read something from the way the dust felt in her fingers.

The woman was amazing. There was no way she would ever be interested in a man like him—nothing to offer, no place to call home and one screw up away from being unemployed. More than that, she seemed like the kind of woman who liked being on her own—except when she'd seen the other rangers.

She looked up at him, her green eyes nearly the same color as the moss growing on the trees that littered the ground. "These are griz tracks. More than one—the scent of death must have brought them in. I'm guessing it was probably from some-time in the last twenty-four hours."

That's exactly what they needed. Not one, but two hungry grizzlies in the woods near them. In the deep underbrush, it was more than possible that they could run into one. Hopefully it wasn't a sow with cubs. They'd never make it out alive.

Maybe that was what had happened to the hiker—one misstep in the woods; a hike that had started out as some kind of goal or dream and then ended in tragedy.

"Be careful," he said, moving closer to her.

Her mouth quirked into a sexy smirk, but she instinctively reached down and touched the plastic trigger of the bear spray at her waist. "If I go out by bear, at least I'll go out fighting."

He didn't doubt her, but he could have sworn

he saw a flicker of fear in her eyes. Then again, anyone who came into these woods and didn't pay heed to the place's ability to take them out at the knees was a fool. And maybe it was just that type of fool whose body they were trying to locate.

A branch snapped and his attention jerked toward the unnerving noise. The sound came from higher up the mountain, as if something was moving through the dense forest in a hurry. He could only hope whatever had made the sound was moving away.

Alexis was motionless, but her body was tense as though she had kicked into fight or flight.

"It's okay," he said, trying to calm her fears while at the same time trying to conquer his own. "Whatever made that sound is long gone." He waved almost too dismissively.

She glanced over at him, and her frown reappeared. "If there's an animal up there, it means there might be more of the body. We need to look."

He paused. The last thing he wanted to do was end up like the victim they were trying to identify, but he didn't want to come off like a coward to the sexy, dark-haired Alexis. "I'll take point. Watch my six," he said, trying not to think about the job he'd volunteered for as he followed the deep gouges up the hillside in the direction of the terrifying noise.

On a small patch of melting snow a square of army-green cloth caught his eye. He moved toward the object, unsure of whether or not the thing was really something worth looking at or just another green splotch in nature's underbelly.

Moving closer, he knelt down so he could make out the square lines and straps of a backpack, the kind that could be found at any of a million surplus supply stores. There was a smear of blood on the bag, near the right shoulder strap. Before he touched it, he motioned for Alexis to take photos. She snapped a few, carefully documenting the scene.

She stuffed the camera back into her pocket and knelt down beside him just as his knees started to grow damp in the snow. She gingerly picked the pack up by its straps and set it upright.

Opening up the bag's top flap, the bag was filled with clear, square packages of drugs. She took out the bricks and one by one laid them on the only dry spot she could find, a downed log, and took pictures of each item with a scale.

"Holy…" he whispered. "How many bricks are there?"

"Ten," Alexis said. "You have any idea about what kind of drugs these are?"

He leaned in closer, and through the cloudy plastic he could make out hundreds of blue pills.

"Without a drug test kit I can't be a hundred percent sure, but I know they ain't Viagra." His face flamed as he realized what he had said to her, and he instinctively glanced to the hand he had held.

She giggled, like she had been able to read his thoughts, and the heat rose higher in his face.

He held his head low, fearing that if he looked in her direction she would be able to see how embarrassed he was, but instead of studying him, she reached in the bag and pulled out the last brick and documented it.

She flipped the bag over. At the bottom was a wad of cash, at least a thousand dollars, held together by a thick rubber band.

"How do you think the bag got up here? You think the bears stole it?" she asked with a slight laugh at her twisted joke.

"You know of any bears that need a thousand bucks and some drugs?"

She laughed again, the sound fluttering through the air like a rare butterfly, and just as quickly as it had come, it disappeared.

"But really, either the guy dropped it when he was running or…" He picked up the bag and showed her the claw marks. He flipped it so she could see the dark bloodstains that were speckled over its surface. "This is definitely arterial spray.

Which means this guy must have been carrying this when he was mauled."

She shrugged. "It definitely could have been a mauling. It wouldn't be the first and I doubt it will be the last, but something about this whole thing—maybe it's the drugs—it just doesn't feel right. There has to be something more, something we're missing."

He felt it, too, the strange charge in the air that came with a great case. "Do you think someone murdered this guy, Alexis?"

"Call me Lex," she said, interrupting him. "My friends…they call me Lex." A faint tinge of pink rose in her cheeks.

He smiled. So they were friends, just as he had hoped.

"Anyway…what were you saying?" she asked, her voice soft and coy.

That place deep inside him—that place in his heart he often pushed aside for logic and reason—reawakened.

"I…I guess I was just saying that you might be right was all… I mean, if I was a killer and I wanted to hide a body, this is one heck of a place to do it. It's late in the season. It would be easy enough to bring a person up here, shoot them and leave them to be reabsorbed by nature. Another few days and no one would have been back up here until next year. It could have been a nearly perfect attempt at a murder and cover-up."

She nibbled her bottom lip, and it made him wonder what it felt like to kiss those lips. They were so perfect, pink and full, even a little sun-tanned from all her hours hiking. He ran his tongue over his lip and gave it a slight suck as his mind wandered to more sultry thoughts of all the places of hers he would like to kiss.

"How do you know that's arterial blood?" she asked, motioning toward the stain on the bag.

He forced himself to look away from her mouth. "Arterial blood spatter tends to have a redder color, and the droplets are small or medium because they are expelled from the body at a higher speed."

Her face pulled into a tight pucker and she looked up the mountain. "You thinking it could be from a bullet?"

He shrugged. "Without having the medical examiner go over the foot, and without more of the body…well, it's hard to say exactly what might have happened. Maybe it wouldn't be a bad idea if we go get Travis and the other guys."

"No," she clipped. "We don't need Travis. We'll be fine."

There was definitely something between her and this Travis guy. Jealousy zinged through him.

She snapped another quick picture of the drugs

and the money, and stuffed everything back into the bag before she stood up. "Let's keep moving up the mountain. Maybe we'll find the rest of whomever this belongs to. If we do, it's possible we can get a few more questions answered."

Maybe it was selfish, or adolescent, or whatever his therapist would've called it, but what he really wanted more than to find this body—and open whatever can of questions it would entail—was to spend more time with Lex. Their time together was the first real human contact he'd had all summer. Sure, he'd seen hikers and tourists, but their interactions had been little beyond looking at passports and the normal small talk.

In the deepening shadows, they picked their way up the hill into larger and larger clumps of snow, which made their tracking easier. A squirrel chirped overhead, making him jump.

"There," she said, pointing toward a reddish patch on the snow. "Look…"

There, half-buried in the snow, was a yellow patch of bone. On its surface were smears of blood. His stomach dropped. Hopefully he'd been wrong about this being a murder. Hopefully this was nothing more than a mauling. A death was always a terrible thing, but if this was a murder the ramifications would play out until the case was solved, and the deeper the investigation would go, the deeper he would be forced to go into his former world—a world he had promised to leave behind.

Alexis carefully snapped a picture and documented the scene. She pulled on a pair of latex gloves, and reached down and picked up the bone that was buried in the snow. The bone was round and, where it wasn't tacky with blood, it was oily from fat.

It could have been his years of seeing the dead, but as he watched her work to gently move the heavy, wet remains from the ice that had formed around it, he wasn't thinking about the life that this bit of flesh had once belonged to; rather, all he could think about was Lex and the way her face had paled the second her fingers had touched the bone.

"You don't have to stay, Lex. You can go get the guys," he offered. "I can handle this."

She shook her head and wiped the back of her sleeve over her forehead.

"Seriously, Lex. You don't have to do this."

"No. I'm fine," she said, but her voice was weaker than what he was sure she had intended it to be. "This is my job. I got it."

Ever so gently, he reached over and took the bone from her.

She gave an appreciative sigh. "Do you think… it is him?"

"It could be," he said. He slowly turned the bone.

Lex gasped.

In his hands, barely discernible thanks to the jagged holes and chew marks, was the partial face of what had once been a man.

Chapter Three

The coroner laid the skull down on the black body bag. There was a patch of hair, dark with dried blood and grease, and an ear that hung limp, tethered by only a thin strip of pale skin. "Look at this mark right here," he said, pointing to a jagged, round wound at the base of the man's skull. "If this was the entrance of a bullet wound, it would be smooth around the edges, and depending on the angle, there would be a large exit wound."

"So this wasn't a homicide?" Casper asked as he leaned in closer to look at the mark on the bone.

"If you look right here," Hal said, "the margins of the wound are jagged. It's the type you normally see associated with a high-pressure compression wound, consistent with that of a bite. However, without the rest of the body, it's hard to say if this wound was the cause of death or was caused antemortem, perimortem or postmortem."

She looked away. To get through this she had to think of him as just another man. A random being. A victim of the fates. It was nature.

"Are you okay?" Casper asked, putting his hand on the small of her back.

She swallowed a bit of bile that had managed to sneak through her resolve. "I'm fine," she said, her voice hoarse.

Hal zipped up the bag, hiding the gruesome head from view. "I'll get this to the medical examiner. Maybe he can tell us a little more, but for now I'm going to rule the cause of death as undetermined. Don't be surprised if this comes back as being likely due to unintentional injuries. This bite," he said, motioning toward the bag at his feet, "would have been fatal." He stood up and wiped off the knees of his pants.

Travis tapped Hal on the shoulder, drawing his attention. "You ready? The pilot is starting to get antsy."

Hal nodded. "You guys need a ride out?"

Casper took a step toward the copter, but Lex stopped him as she looked over at Travis. The last place she wanted to be was sitting next to her ex-husband in a flying death machine. "Thanks, but we'll hike out."

"Are you sure? Alexis, I think you should get back to the station—" Travis started to protest, but stopped as if he had realized, a moment too late, that he no longer had control over her. "Or do whatever. You never listened to me anyway."

It wasn't that she hadn't listened, it was simply that she wasn't the kind of woman who was ever going to have her actions dictated to her—especially not by someone who had once said that he loved her. "Would you and John let the other rangers know that we have a possible dangerous bear?" She carefully sidestepped his jab. "We're going to need to send up the biologists and a ranger in the morning to track this bear down. We don't need any more tourists getting hurt."

"Maybe you should worry about yourself," Travis grumbled, glancing over toward Casper.

Casper smiled, the motion so wide that it made her wonder if he had misunderstood Travis's tone. "Don't worry about Alexis," he said, motioning toward her. "She'll be safe with me."

Travis gave a tight nod and turned away, muttering unintelligibly under his breath.

Watching him walk away, she was filled with mixed emotions. She thought of the first time she'd met Travis. It had been her first day at work, he had been so kind in showing her around and when she'd gotten a headache, he'd driven three hours to get her Tylenol. At first he had been so good at the little things, the love notes and wildflowers left on the counter. Yet after a couple of years, things progressively got worse and she hated him and what he had done to her, the way he had always put her down and treated her like she was less-than. Then again, such hate could only come at the cost of having once loved.

Casper looked over at her, and she tightened her jaw in an attempt to hide her thoughts from leaking into her expression. She didn't need him asking her any questions about her past. "Thanks for everything, Hal. And please let me know how it all turns out," she said, giving the coroner a quick wave.

"No problem. But wait, what about the drugs?" Hal asked, motioning toward the backpack at Casper's feet.

"This whole thing's going into evidence once we get down," Casper said.

"You sure you don't want me to take them with us? I can drop them off in evidence for you. Would save you a couple pounds carrying it out," Travis said.

She would carry a thousand pounds just so long as she never had to ask for Travis's help. "Nope. We got it," she clipped.

"My team's at your disposal if you need," Hal added and then quickly made his way to the helicopter, disappearing behind its doors. She reached down and took Casper's hand and pulled him, urging him to follow. His hand was hot in hers and she let go, the touch a jolt to her cold, exposed skin. Casper looked at her, a shocked expression on his face like he was surprised that she had touched him, but she pretended not to notice.

Hopefully Travis was watching and could see that no matter how they had left things, she was moving on with her life.

The helicopter lifted off the ground, the wash sending bits of dust and debris in every direction. Travis sent her a look through the copter's window as he said something on his radio.

Casper turned toward her. "You do realize that now we're going to have to hike out…in the dark."

"That's the easy part," she said with a wicked smile.

He raised an eyebrow in question.

"The hard part," she teased, "is that you won't be able to beat me." She took off with a laugh, relieved that once again she was alone with the cowboy.

THE CBP's CHEVY always seemed to list to the left when he drove down the road, and it squealed when he applied the brakes, but as they got to the bottom of the trail, he had never been happier to see his old, beat-up, Fed-issued truck.

"You're crazy. You know that, right?" Casper said between heaving breaths.

He'd thought five miles uphill going in was bad, but basically jogging five miles down steep terrain carrying not only his go-bag, but also the missing hiker's drugs, had nearly killed him.

Even in the light of his flashlight he could make out the beads of sweat that were dripping down Lex's temples. Her hair was damp and her cheeks were red, but she laughed like her body couldn't be aching as badly as his. "Come on, that was fun."

"Having a heart attack is never fun. You could've killed me. I'm getting old, you know."

She lifted her brow, giving him a sexy "come on now" look. Reaching into her bag, she pulled out two protein bars and handed him one. "Here. Eat this, old man. It'll make you feel better."

He took it, dropping his bags on the tailgate of his truck parked at the trailhead. She lifted her bag up and set it beside his.

He looked over at her and tried to guess at her age. She was young; the lines on her face were barely defined in the thin light, but she had the eyes of a woman who had had her heart broken more times than once. "How old are you?"

"Young enough to be okay with it, but old enough to know not to answer," she said, her sexy smirk returning.

He laughed, and some of his tiredness disappeared. "You wanna ride back to Apgar with me or do you want me to drop you off at the nearest station?"

She dropped her hand down on her backpack. "Apgar would be great. I don't want to have to wait for another ranger so I can catch a ride." She looked down at her watch.

"You don't want to have to wait for another ranger, or is it that you don't want to run into Travis?"

Her face puckered at the man's name and he instantly regretted asking her the question.

"Sorry. Don't answer that. It's none of my business. Let's go." He slammed closed the tailgate and the topper. He jumped into the truck before she had a chance to answer.

After a minute she dropped into the seat beside him. They drove in silence for what seemed like an hour.

"How'd you know about Travis?" she finally asked.

"I was in the FBI for five years. Let's just say I've learned how to read people."

"If you're so good at reading people, then how did you end up working at Goat Haunt? I thought only loners and outcasts liked that station. Last year it was manned by some lady...Gertrude or something. I swear the only word that woman ever said to me was, 'Passport?'" Lex's voice was soft, like she was trying to avoid hurting his feelings, but the blade had already sliced.

She was right. Goat Haunt was his own private version of Alcatraz.

"What can I say, I guess I'm just lucky," he said, trying to make light of the situation.

He steered the truck around the sharp corners and down the narrow road of the Going-to-the-Sun Highway. The moon had risen and made it just bright enough that he could make out the snow-capped peaks of the jagged mountains around them. To their left was a steep drop-off; the only thing standing in the way of a car going over and plummeting hundreds of feet to the bottom of the mountain was a short rock wall.

He forced himself to focus on the road and ignore the tight knot of fear that always filled his gut when he came this way. At least the park was closed for the night, so there were only a few other cars—those that dared to spend the night in the park, or were hurrying to get out.

"I'm sorry. I shouldn't have said that," Alexis started. "I...I'm just a little touchy when it comes to Travis. He's my ex-husband. Lately things haven't been going well between us."

He knew all about exes. He'd had more than his

fair share, but after the events that had transpired with the FBI, he'd taken the last two years off from dating. It was his way of protecting another person from getting hurt. Yet when he looked at Alexis, he was tempted to break his self-imposed vow of celibacy. There was just something about the tomboy next to him. She wasn't the type of woman who worried about a broken nail. She was the type who would be happy hanging out, reading a book, maybe going for a hike—and no matter how he counted it, spontaneous and real were always a turn-on. No matter how badly he didn't want them to be.

"You want to talk about it?" he asked, trying to avoid looking at her hand resting between them on the bench seat.

She shook her head. "What about you? I noticed you don't have a ring."

"It's a long story," he said, casting a look at her.

"I heard that kind of thing has been going around." She smiled. "Relationships are tricky— when you think you have a good one, it's easy to get complacent and take things for granted, and with bad ones you are always struggling to find an escape."

His thoughts moved to his parents and how tricky their relationship had been. They hated one another and had fought every day when he'd been growing up. Though they were still married, the thought of the relationship they had made the word *marriage* sour on his tongue.

Though he didn't like the thought of marriage—at least the type of marriage he'd seen as a child—he still held hope that one day he'd find something different. Yet from the way Lex spoke, he wasn't sure if she was attempting to make him feel better, or if it was a way of telling him she wasn't interested. Either way, whatever residual hopes he had held in making something out of their clandestine meeting were gone.

A roar grew loud behind them. In the rearview mirror was a single headlight.

Alexis leaned forward and peered into the side mirror. "Who'd be crazy enough to drive a motorcycle down this thing at night?"

Besides the cliffs and the sheer drop-offs, Glacier was known for the goats and random assortments of animals that loved to use the highway as their own personal travel system, avoiding the steep embankments and treacherous climbs.

"Maybe that's why they want to hug my bumper," he said, checking the mirror. The bike was now so close to their tailgate that he could no longer see the headlight—it was nothing more than a reflective glow.

He moved to slow down, but as he did, so did

the biker, moving back so far that he lost track of the headlight around a corner.

"What's that guy doing?" Alexis asked, a whisper of fear creeping into her voice.

"Who knows, but don't worry. We're fine. The guy's probably just drunk or something." Casper had driven this road a few times over the summer, but normally when he got off work he'd just avoid the park and drive home to the tiny town of Babb outside the park, where he had a little apartment on the second floor of a local auto mechanics shop. "Where's the next pullout?"

Alexis shook her head. "Not for a mile or two."

He was blinded as a car turned the corner ahead. It was moving fast and hugging the center line of the narrow road. He gripped the steering wheel, his fingers digging into the hard vinyl.

At the last moment, the car swerved into their lane. He jerked the wheel, running the truck off the road and toward the rock wall.

He reached across the truck, trying to stop Lex from lurching forward, but there was nothing he could do. The old Chevy's tires squealed as the steel body ran against an outcrop of unyielding stone in a mess of metal and sparks.

The truck's tire caught and, almost in slow motion, it twisted. The world shifted and what had once been up was now down. As they slid to a stop, the truck was lying on its roof. Lex was held in place by her seat belt, her body slumped against the straps and her eyes closed. Blood dripped down her hair and fell onto the gray roof.

"Alexis? Lex?" he called frantically, hoping she was still alive. "Lex, are you okay?"

He started to move, but his strap held him in place upside down. The blood started to rush to his head, making his face feel heavy and bloated. Reaching up, he tried to unclasp his belt, but his fingers fumbled as he tried to make them work.

The deafening beat of his heart started to slow and as he looked at Lex his vision distorted, making her look as though she were a picture going out of focus. His vision tunneled until he could only see her face. A wave of peace filled him.

If this was it, the last thing he was going to see—her long hair and full lips—he could think of no greater goodbye.

Chapter Four

Alexis opened her eyes. The world was awash with the sounds of frantic voices. She didn't know where she was; the world floated around her, moving and swaying like she was watching it through a pool of water.

"Alexis?" A man's voice broke through her thoughts. "Are you okay? Lex?"

She blinked and there, kneeling beside her, was Casper with his silver badge on his belt and hair the color of chestnut, reds and browns that reflected the lights that filled the night, and shoulders so muscular that she was certain he did push-ups as a hobby. As he looked at her, his eyes were wide with fear.

She tried to speak, but nothing more than a slight squeak escaped her lips. Her head ached and as she drew a breath, her chest ached. Swallowing back the pain, she tried again to speak. "What…happened?"

Casper leaned closer and moved her hair out of her face. The strands stuck to her skin and she moved to reach up, but he stopped her. Then she tasted the blood. It filled her mouth, giving it the iron-rich taste of spilled life.

"Don't worry. You're going to be okay. The EMTs are almost here. It's just important that you stay awake. Got it?" He spoke in fast, clipped words that she struggled to understand.

"How?" she asked, groping for the words that seemed to jumble in her mind.

"We were in a car accident."

It all came flooding back. The car flipping through the air. The screech of metal on stone. The scent of gas in the air. She drew in a gasp, but was stopped by the pain in her chest.

She tried to sit up, but stopped as Casper shook his head. "Don't move."

A thin bead of blood slipped down Casper's hairline and stopped next to his earlobe. "Are you okay?" she asked.

He nodded, reaching up and wiping the blood away, leaving a streak of red on his cheek. "I'm fine."

In the group of people beside Casper there was a man staring at her. He wore a black leather vest with the words "Madness and Mayhem." Just below them was the word "Montana" and then a black patch with red stitching that read "Filthy Few." On the other side of the man's vest was a patch that read "one-percenter." The man had gray hair and even though it was dark, he had on sunglasses.

The man must have noticed her looking at him, as he lifted his chin in acknowledgment. This must have been the man who had been following them, the headlight in the mirror. Yet before she could speak, someone stepped in front of him and the man disappeared, becoming just another face in the growing crowd.

On the rock wall beside them she could see the glow of red and blue lights. Tires crunched on the side of the road as the EMTs pulled to a stop.

"Everyone out of the way!" the paramedic yelled as she pushed her way through people.

The EMTs poked and prodded Alexis, taking her pulse and checking her reflexes with lights. Even without them telling her, she knew everything wasn't right. She closed her eyes and when she reopened them she was already strapped down to a board, her head and back immobile, and they were loading her into the back of the ambulance.

"Casper..." Alexis whispered as the female

EMT stepped up into the back of the ambulance beside her.

"What, honey?" the EMT asked.

"Where's Casper?"

"Your friend?"

Alexis tried to nod, but was stopped by the thick straps on her forehead. "Yes. I want Casper."

The woman jumped out of the wagon and a moment later, Casper was sitting beside Alexis. He smiled. The blood on his temple had dried. "I'm here."

There was so much going on. So much she didn't understand. "Stay with me," she pleaded, suddenly afraid.

"Don't worry, sweetheart, I'm not going anywhere. I'll stay by your side as long as you need."

HE'D SEEN MORE people hurt than he could count, but he'd never felt as terrified as when he saw Alexis covered in blood and confused. Hopefully she would be okay. She was so out of it.

She slept as they waited for the doctor to return with the results of her MRI. He hated the monotonous, shrill beeps of the machines that filled the emergency room.

Reaching into the plastic bag at his feet, he pulled out the little sewing kit he'd bought at the hospital's shop and grabbed her pants from the foot of her bed. He pushed his fingers through the L-shaped hole in her pant leg from where she had caught it on the deadfall. She probably didn't care about the pants, but he couldn't sit there with nothing to do but worry.

He pulled out some string, threaded the needle and set to work as he sat in the pink vinyl seat beside her bed. When he'd been younger, his mother had told him that good domestic skills were the mark of a true man.

The stitches were even and as he mended, he kept looking up, hoping Lex would wake and everything would be okay.

He hated this. He hated hospitals—it brought up moments of his past that he never wanted to relive. The sooner they could be out of here, the better.

Every hospital he'd ever been to carried the same overpowering disinfectant smell. They could scrub away the blood and the waste products, but no matter how much they tried to hide it, he could still make out the pungent aroma of panic and fear. Yet as he sat there working, he wondered if the scent was carrying in from the patients or from those waiting for their loved ones to be helped.

He reached over and caressed Lex's hand. There was no more fear for her, not now, not with the drugs that filtered through her system to numb her pain. Now the fear was solely his.

His phone buzzed. "Hello?"

"Agent Lawrence, this is Ranger Grant with the Glacier National Park Rangers Office. I was one of the responders at the scene of your accident. I believe you left me a message?"

"Thanks for returning my call. I appreciate it," Casper said. "Did you manage to find the evidence?"

There was a pause on the other end of the line. "We found two large hiking backpacks—which I assumed were yours and Alexis's—and there was an empty green military-style bag."

"Empty?"

"Yep."

"You've got to be kidding me. You sure there wasn't anything in the bag?" He pulled a hand over his face, trying to stave off the start of a headache.

"Yes, sir."

"The drugs were packed into bricks. Were there any that had spilled out? Maybe into the truck bed or on scene?" He tried to sound calm as he thought about what it would mean if the drugs were truly missing.

"I didn't find any bricks of drugs, but your topper took a pretty big hit when you rolled the truck." The man paused. "When we pulled up, the truck's topper door was open. I guess it's possible they fell out and weren't recovered."

"Or they were taken…"

His mind raced. Who'd want to take the drugs? Only a few people had even known that they had them and were taking them back to Apgar. Was it possible that the coroner or one of the rangers had said something? Or was it completely a random occurrence that they had been in an accident and the drugs had been stolen?

He didn't believe in coincidences, but he had a hard time believing that the rangers or the coroner would have any ill-conceived ideas of stealing the drugs. No one had seemed overly preoccupied with them on the scene. If someone had wanted them, Casper would have had some type of clue. He was jumping to conclusions… No doubt the drugs were probably scattered along the roadside near their crash site.

"Can you make a run back up to the site? Take another look around? We can't have thousands of dollars' worth of drugs get into the wrong hands."

"No problem… I'll call you when I get back into cell service and let you know what I find."

Casper squeezed Lex's hand. It had started to chill under the hospital's air-conditioning and he carefully tucked her arms under the warm blanket.

"Thanks, Grant," he said. "Appreciate your help." He moved to hang up.

"Wait, Lawrence," the man said.

He lifted the phone back to his ear. "Huh?"

"We did find a receipt inside the green bag. It was wadded into a ball and was stuck in the bottom corner."

A receipt? He thought back to everything he'd dumped out of the bag. He didn't recall a receipt. Was it possible it had been there the whole time, or had the person who'd stolen the drugs accidentlly, or purposefully, left it behind?

"What about the money?"

"No money. Just the receipt," Grant said, sounding tired. "I'll take a picture and send it your way."

"Thanks, Grant."

"No problem. We'll start putting out feelers. If the drugs were stolen, maybe we can help you try to get a handle on this before word moves up the chain. Hate to see you get in trouble."

"Let me know if you hear anything." He hung up the phone.

He moved too fast as he pushed through another stitch and the needle jabbed into his finger, making him curse as he pushed his finger into his mouth to stem the blood flow.

He was going to be in deep trouble if the news that he'd fallen victim to a heist hit the Fed circuit. If it did, within twenty-four hours everyone from his boss to his old FBI buddies would know that he'd lost a vital piece of evidence.

Just when he thought things couldn't get any worse.

He knotted the thread as he finished mending the hole and then put everything away.

He was going to need to get in touch with his boss. He glanced down at his watch. Midnight. No wonder Grant had been tired.

Instead of calling and waking up the captain, he wrote him a bare-bones email that emphasized the fact he was sitting in the ER. It was low, playing the mercy card, but he needed to buy some time and a little leniency. The last thing he needed his boss thinking was that he lost the drugs due to his incompetence.

The door to Lex's room opened, but with the curtain drawn around her bed he couldn't see who was coming in.

"Is this the right place?" a man asked, his voice tight and filled with panic.

"It is, Mr...." a woman answered.

"Yellowfeather. Travis Yellowfeather."

Casper's heart lurched in his chest. What was Lex's ex-husband doing here?

He looked down at her sleeping face and contemplated waking her. Yet she looked so peaceful, her eyes fluttering with REM sleep and her hair, still specked with blood, haloed around her head. She needed her rest.

"Mr. Yellowfeather, I'm afraid she already has a visitor. We only allow one visitor at a time," the nurse said.

"To hell with one visitor," Travis said, pushing aside the curtain.

As soon as he saw Casper, Travis's eyes darkened and his lips curled into a smirk. "I should've known it was you who would be here. I guess it wasn't enough that you got her hurt, now you have to stay here to make sure she doesn't die—all in an effort to save your conscience, I suppose."

Casper went slack-jawed, but he quickly recovered his composure. "Who do you think you are, Travis, walking in here and accusing me of anything?"

"I'm her damned husband," he retorted, moving to the side of Alexis's bed.

"Ex, from what I hear."

Travis's scowl darkened. "She told you?" He snorted. "So she's already on the prowl," he said, half under his breath.

"Why don't you leave, Travis? I know she wouldn't want you here."

"And you think she wants you?" His scowl turned into a dangerous smile. "If you think that, you don't know Lex at all."

Travis wasn't wrong. He couldn't tell anyone Alexis's favorite sandwich or the color of her childhood bedroom, but that didn't mean he was going to leave her here with the man whom, only hours before, she shied away from. He knew fear and hatred when he saw it.

"If you think she would want you here, then I may know her better than you do," Casper said.

Lex's hand tightened in his and he turned to see her eyes fluttering open. "Boys," she said, her voice weak, "don't fight."

Travis pulled his lips into a tight line, but he shut up.

"How are you doing, honey?" Casper asked. He moved to caress her face but stopped as he felt Travis's gaze searing into him. Lex didn't need a fight, and no matter how much he disliked the man standing at the other side of the bed, he had been right—Casper barely knew her. They had talked a lot as they hiked, and there had been playful banter, but they were only friends.

She blinked for a few moments, as if trying to make sense of her world. "What are you doing here, Trav?"

Travis stepped closer to her and took her other hand. "I heard you were in an accident."

He suddenly felt out of place as Alexis said her ex-husband's pet name. Maybe he'd misread the entire situation. Maybe she didn't hate Travis like he'd assumed. He let go. He was the interloper here, not Travis.

"But why are you here?" She moved her hand out of Travis's. Casper hoped she would reach over for him, but she remained still. "You and I are done. You made that abundantly clear."

"We may be divorced, Lex, but that doesn't mean that I can just stop worrying about you."

She pushed the button that moved the bed up. "Actually, Travis, that's exactly what a divorce means. If that's not what you wanted, then maybe you should have treated me like your wife instead of just someone you could use and throw away."

Casper cleared his throat, his discomfort rising. He shouldn't have come here and inserted himself into whatever domestic situation they had going on. "Hey, Lex, I'll see you later."

"No," she said, her voice strong. "You stay here. Travis, it's you who needs to go."

"Are you kidding me?" Travis spat. "You are going to let this son of a—"

Alexis stopped him with a wave of her hand. "Just go."

Travis looked at her and started to open his mouth to say something, but must have thought better of it. He turned to Casper. "You think she's great now, but let me tell you a little something about Alexis Finch. She only cares about two things—

the park and how she fits into it. She doesn't care about anyone or anything else. If you think you are going to change her or if you got some notion that you are going to be someone she gives two shakes about…" He snorted. "You got another thing coming." He turned and stalked out of the ER, rattling the curtain rings as he bulled through them.

Casper stood in silence, staring at the curtain. He had no idea what to say. Divorce was never pretty—especially when it came to navigating the waters of a new relationship. Not that they had a relationship, but things could get a bit hinky when it came to seeing an ex with someone else.

"I'm sorry about that," Lex said. She tried to move her head, but it was still in the confines of a brace and as she moved, she winced.

"Are you okay?"

"I'm fine," she said, the tired edge returning to her voice.

"I'm serious, I can go, Lex. I don't want to… interfere."

Her lips turned into a thin smile. "You made a promise. You said you would stay by my side, remember?"

He moved closer to her bed. He thought about reaching down and taking her hand, but now that Travis had been there somehow it didn't seem right.

"How're you feeling?"

"I feel like I was in a fight… Who won, me or the truck?" Her lips curled into a playful half smile.

There was a knock on the door and the doctor pushed back the curtain. He had a black tablet hugged to his white lab coat.

"Mrs. Finch?" he asked.

"Miss," she answered.

"Right, Ms. Finch, I'm Dr. Tag, the neurologist here at Kalispell Regional. I just got off the phone with your brother, Dr. Paul Finch. He was very concerned about your well-being."

She cringed at the sound of her brother's name. "I'm sorry, Doctor, he can be a bit…overwhelming sometimes."

Dr. Tag didn't smile or nod, rather, he remained unflappable, making Casper wonder if that was exactly what had drawn the man to medicine.

"It was no problem, Ms. Finch, but you should call him back when you get the chance. I think he wishes to speak to you regarding your accident now that you're awake."

She nodded but looked down at her hands.

"As for the results of your CAT scan, you are experiencing a slight bit of swelling, consistent with a mild concussion."

"What does that mean, Doc?" Casper asked, trying to mimic the man's cool demeanor.

"It means that for the time being, I'd like to have you stay here and be monitored for any residual effects. However, I think it would be safe to send you home tomorrow. You will just need to rest and everything should sort itself out." He tapped on his tablet like he was noting something in her chart. "You are a lucky woman. A TBI, or a traumatic brain injury, can have a number of long-term effects, but from what I'm seeing on your scans, you should be okay."

Casper let out a breath he hadn't known he was holding. In a day that had been filled with nothing but death, despair, accidents and blood…something was finally going right.

Chapter Five

Lex took a tentative step out of the car as Casper raced around from the driver's side to help her into her house. He wrapped his arm around her waist and took hold of her arm as he cradled her body against him. He was so…warm. In fact, he was so warm that she wanted to move closer to him, to rest her body against him and let his heat ease the pain that seemed to pulse from her bruised and battered body. He smelled of hospital, but beneath the sharp odor of antiseptic was the heady scent of his sweat and the tangy edge of fresh air. She closed her eyes and took his scent deep into her lungs, trying to remember it for those nights that she would be alone.

"Do you need anything for your house? Groceries? Anything?" Casper asked.

"No, uh, I think I got everything I need." She looked over at him as she spoke and saw his face was tight, just like it had been when the doctor had been in her hospital room last night. It was sweet that he was so worried about her, but he needn't be; she was strong. "Thanks for giving me a ride—and for keeping the car on the road this time," she joked, trying to make light of the accident.

Her joke fell flat as his brow furrowed and a storm brewed in his eyes. "I'm so sorry, Lex. I...I never wanted you to get hurt—"

She stopped him by pressing her finger to his lips. The instant she touched him, a strange buzz of energy filled her and she quickly lowered her hand. "You—it wasn't your fault. It was unavoidable. That car came at us. Seriously, don't worry. Everything is fine. And hey, at least it was a work truck, right?" She struggled to find the right words to make him feel better, and to quell the surging need to touch him again.

He looked at her and some of the darkness in his eyes lifted. Before he could say anything, she stepped out of his cradling arms and hurried toward her house.

The log cabin was dark brown and its windows were trimmed with white, and like most of the other buildings of the park, it radiated with a cozy, rustic charm that always beckoned her home. She'd spent the last few summers holed up in the tiny building with Travis, often hating its inconsistent hot water and the electricity that seemed to come and go depending on the weather, but regardless of its downfalls she loved the place.

Yet it felt strange walking up the path with a man who wasn't Travis. In fact, the night he'd left, she had sworn that, as long as she lived there, he would be the last man who would ever set foot in this place. Then again, Casper wasn't anything like Travis.

He was handsome…maybe even a little too handsome for her liking. Every nurse who had come into her room had kept their eyes on him a moment too long. It had been tempting to show the women that he was hers, but the truth was just the opposite. He was nothing more than a work colleague…albeit a work colleague who hadn't left her side since the accident.

More than simply being handsome, he had a kind side. Often he tried to act tough, all business, but when he'd stepped between her and Travis in the hospital she had caught a glimpse of the sensitive and caring side that he tried to hide from the world.

She glanced over at him, but his face was hidden in the shadow cast by his hat. Maybe she was wrong; maybe she had an idealized version of who he really was—she had a terrible habit of doing that. She had sworn Travis was her knight in shining armor. At first it hadn't mattered that her friends had warned her off; it didn't matter when he told her who she could be friends with and what time she should come home, and it didn't matter that for days on end he treated her like she was nothing more than his often neglected pet…coming and going as he pleased and not speaking to her for days. All that had mattered was that when he looked at her, the world stood still.

If only she had listened to what everyone had told her, and that tiny place in the back of her mind that had told her it was all too good to be true.

She couldn't risk being hurt like that again. She doubted she could live through it a second time. "What did you do before you got stationed at Goat Haunt?" she asked as she unlocked the door.

Casper tensed at the question. He was so quiet that she wondered if he had even heard her.

"Casper?"

"Yeah… I was in the FBI. Mostly specializing toward the end—handwriting analysis, that kind of thing." He closed the door behind them and stood there, his back to her as he stared at the door like a trapped animal.

"Look, if you want, you can go. I think I can handle things from here."

He took out his phone and glanced down at his screen. "No…it's fine. Grant hasn't gotten back to me yet. There's nothing more for me to do until I hear from him."

"What all did he say?" she asked as she gingerly walked to the old, tattered brown couch and sat down. There was a threadbare quilt that hung over the back, one her foster mother had made her back in grade school. There was even a bit of purple nail polish she had carelessly spilled ages ago.

"The drugs are missing. He's going to go back to the scene and check to make sure he didn't miss anything." Stuffing the phone into the breast pocket of his jean jacket, he sat down in the recliner across from her. "And he found a receipt."

"A receipt? What do you mean?"

"It was jammed into the corner of the green bag."

"I swear I looked everywhere in that thing… But I guess I could have missed it. Wait, do you think someone planted it, Mr. FBI?"

He cringed, but she wasn't sure why.

He opened up his phone and pulled up the photos of the bag that they had taken on scene. "Regardless of how it got there, because we screwed up the chain of custody, the receipt can't be used in court for anything. We can't prove that it was or wasn't there without reasonable doubt."

"But it could help us figure out the vic's identity, right?"

"I suppose," he said, giving her a weak smile. "Right now though, you need to take care of yourself and just focus on getting some rest." He stood up and grabbed the quilt off the back of the couch, wrapping it around her shoulders.

She caught his familiar scent and closed her eyes. She imagined pulling him down on the couch beside her, wrapping him in the blanket and letting him hold her. They could spend the day together, huddled in each other's embrace and away from the hurt that filled the world around them.

When she opened her eyes to find him looking at her, she started to reach toward him, but he pulled away. She dropped her hand and realized that it was still hidden by the blanket. He couldn't have known what she was thinking or what she wanted, but there was still a pang of rejection.

"Uh, tea or coffee?" he asked with a cute half smile.

By this time of day she was normally on her second or even third cup of the tar-black stuff they brewed at the ranger station. Yet the thought of the melt-your-spoon coffee made her stomach churn. "Tea, but I can get it." She moved to stand up, but he stopped her.

"No. You. Sit. Down," he commanded, pointing at the couch. "I got this."

She did as he asked and he made his way to the kitchen.

There was a bang of cupboards and the sound of water running. She leaned over the arm of the couch, trying to catch a glimpse of what he was doing, but he was just out of sight. "The teapot's on the stove, but if you need a cup—"

"Got it, but where're the tea bags?"

It was her solemn belief the best tea could only be brewed by use of loose leaf teas, but somehow asking him—the man who banged around in her kitchen like a gorilla in its cage—to go to that much work seemed like a stretch. "There's some leftover stuff in the cupboard over the stove," she said as a smile played across her lips.

Somehow it felt right having a man back in the place, someone to share the little space. Then again, over the last year she had found solace in being alone. She could have things her own way and take things at her own pace. There was never anyone there pushing her, making her compromise or check in. She had been truly independent.

Casper poked his head around the corner and lifted up a box of Lipton. "This it?" He smiled, and the simple action made her heart stutter.

She nodded. "Are you sure you don't want help?"

He waved her off. "I got this, Lex. Have faith."

Faith was something she had in limited supply—especially when it came to having faith in a man.

She got up, walked to the kitchen and leaned against the wall, the quilt still wrapped around her shoulders.

Casper had his back to her, and his hips moved with a song that must have only been in his head. She moved to speak, to let him know she was there, but stopped and instead just enjoyed the view of his round, well-muscled derriere shifting under his tight jeans. Maybe she was objectifying the man, but she couldn't help herself. He was a fine specimen.

There was a faint whistle as the kettle started to boil and he turned to grab a cup with string hanging out. He saw her and smiled. "How long have you been standing there?"

"Long enough to know that you might have missed your calling. You should've been a stripper." She laughed, and heat rushed to her face as she realized how bold she sounded. "Sorry..." she quickly offered. "Sometimes the filter between my brain and my mouth malfunctions."

"I don't think my mother would agree with you...at least about the stripper bit." He laughed, the sound rich and thick. "And your filter, or lack of one, is something I happen to like about you. Honesty is always attractive."

The heat intensified in her cheeks. "I…er…" she stumbled as she realized that he thought she was pretty. She didn't know exactly how to respond. "Is the tea ready?"

He poured the water over the tea bag and let it sit for a few seconds before handing it to her.

"Thanks," she said, taking a sip of the boiling hot liquid. The tea was so old it had gone stale, but she swallowed it down. "It's great," she said, her voice so high that she wondered if he could hear her lie.

He lifted a corner of the blanket as it started to slip from her shoulder. As his fingers grazed her skin, she found herself leaning into his hand, wanting more.

"How's your head, filter notwithstanding?" he said, his voice taking on a soft edge.

"I'm good." Aside from the way her head seemed to lighten every time he drew near, she felt fine. "Do you have a picture of the receipt?" she asked, trying to move the conversation away from the way she felt. "Maybe we can pull something from it if the person paid with a card."

The light in his eyes dimmed, like he was slightly disappointed in being drawn back to work, yet she couldn't be drawn into anything more than a friendship with the handsome agent. It was too soon to jump into another relationship. It had been a year, but her heartache was still too fresh to want to step into something that almost certainly would shatter her further.

Casper pulled out his phone and scanned through its pictures. "There's one…it looks like the receipt is for someplace called The Prince and the Pea."

"Really?" She giggled, stepping close so she could see the picture of the receipt. "Oh wait, I know that place. It's on the Waterton side."

Glacier National Park was merely one part of the first International Peace Park, spreading over the American/Canadian border and merging with Waterton Lakes Park in Alberta.

"What kind of shop is it?"

She bit her lip as she tried to remember. "It's just a touristy place. You know, flag cups and Waterton sweatshirts."

He stared at his phone. "He spent thirty-seven bucks."

"In a place like that, that wouldn't go very far. Everything around the park is expensive." She glanced at the phone but the receipt didn't list what was purchased or a credit card number.

"Look," she said, pointing to the time stamp. "It's from three days ago, kinda late in the evening."

His gaze moved to the door as if he was thinking about how badly he wanted to go after their lead.

"Let's go," she offered. "If we don't go, we're missing a chance. Maybe we can find whoever was working and they can give us an ID on whoever this belongs to."

He looked back down at his phone and then up again, studying her. "You're supposed to rest. I'm sure Grant is looking into it."

"Grant is a great guy, and he's many things, but he's not the first one I would go to when a lead needs to be investigated."

In truth, Grant was fine—maybe he was biding his time until he was eligible for retirement, but his heart always seemed to be in the right place. He loved the park, maybe even as much as she did.

She took another sip of the steadily cooling tea and tried to control a pucker as bitterness laced over her tongue. Looking over to her closed bedroom door …if she wasn't careful, she feared that she would fall into old habits—habits that led too quickly to that bedroom.

He took her cup and set it in the kitchen sink. "Sorry about the tea."

She laughed. "How about you buy me a cup in Waterton?"

"Why do I have a feeling that this is an argument I'm not going to win?"

Her like for him grew. In her relationship with Travis, he had never pushed her when she'd made up her mind. It was one of the things she had loved about him—his acceptance of her independent nature. But when things had started to go downhill, his love for her independence had turned into hatred of the thing he had sworn he adored. As much as she had tried to compromise and give up a bit of her freedoms, in the end, his possessiveness had only led to irreparable damage.

Maybe things with Casper would be different—then again, who would want to love her? If life had taught her anything, it was that any time she got close, the people she loved fell away. Love, while it started with promises of milk and honey, only ended in immeasurable pain, and pain like that was something she could live without.

IT WAS A long drive to Waterton and they spent most of it talking about the weather and the mundane events of everyday life—not that Casper minded. It was a nice break from the worry and the guilt he'd felt after the accident. Yet every once in a while he still caught himself looking over at her and making sure that she was all right.

She stared out the window as they drove north on Highway 6 on the Canadian side. Waterton wasn't much farther, and the closer they got the quieter she had become. "Are you okay?" he asked, hoping pain wasn't keeping her silent.

"I'm fine," she answered simply.

"You're being quiet. Should I be worried?"

She looked at him with a tragic smile. "Actually, I was just thinking about the accident."

A pang of guilt drove through him. "I'm sorry. Seriously."

"I know. I don't blame you at all." She waved him off. "I was just thinking about the car that came at us. Did Grant find out anything about the other driver?"

He could still see the car's headlights as it came straight at them, and the tiny "H" emblem at the center of the grille. "The car didn't stop. And no one has come forward with any information about who the driver was of the Honda. Why?"

"You remember the biker behind us?"

"Yeah." His hands tightened on the steering wheel.

"You don't suppose they were working together or something, do you?"

He reached up and ran his fingers through his hair, glancing at his hat resting in the middle of the dashboard. "I doubt it. Very few people knew about the accident up by Kootenai. Even fewer knew what we found, and even less knew what we were planning on doing with the evidence."

She sighed. "I know. But everything about this just feels *off.* You know?" She looked over at him with her big green eyes. As they caught the light, he could just make out the edges of brown at their center.

Travis had been an idiot for letting her go.

He forced himself to ignore the feelings that rose within him.

Lex was right. Something about this entire series of events was amiss. Though it could have been mostly the woman at his side, the woman who had reawakened his heart, the woman who made him question the man he thought he was, that had him the most confused.

He just needed to focus on the investigation. While he wasn't sure that she was correct in her conspiracy theory, he had to admit that there was something wrong with the picture.

"We have to look at this objectively, Lex. Right now there is nothing to prove that there was any real criminal act. For all we know, the drugs flew out of the truck and over the side of the cliff, and the car that came at us…well, maybe the driver just wasn't paying attention."

She gave him a sideways glance. "You know that's crap. If the drugs were still on scene, or even near it, Grant would have found them. Someone took them."

"Okay, let's say that happened. Then what are they planning on doing with the drugs? Why would someone take such a huge risk in stealing them from a Fed?"

"Someone who thought they wouldn't get caught," she said. "Think about it. We're in an accident in a place that is basically off the grid, there's little traffic, at least this time of year, and there's a lot of money to be made."

They had been a perfect target, Fed or not. "Or it may have been nothing more than an opportunistic theft. Maybe whoever picked these drugs up is sitting in their hotel right now, wondering how they got themselves into such a mess. They know that we're going to find them. It's only a matter of time."

"Don't you think you're giving people just a little too much credit in assuming that they feel guilty over this?"

In truth, most days he felt the same way, at least when he'd been deep in the FBI. All he'd seen were the dregs of society. They were everywhere—thieves, con men and murderers. It didn't matter what age, sex or socioeconomic bracket a person found themselves in; human nature and the filth that came along with it didn't change.

Yet what could possibly be behind Lex saying something like that? Who had hurt her so bad that she thought the world was only full of evil?

"All I'm saying is that sooner or later we're going to track down these drugs," she continued. "Either someone's going to talk or the drugs are going to start hitting the streets. If they start moving around Montana, we'll hear about it from the local law enforcement."

He cringed at the thought of more agencies joining the chase. It would be a pissing contest in no time and at the center of it all would be him and what some would undoubtedly call his incompetence. "I hope we can figure this problem out long before we get to that point."

He pulled the car to a stop in front of The Prince and the Pea. The place was definitely a tourist shop, its brightly lit windows filled with everything from books to blankets.

Casper walked around the car to help Lex, but she was standing tall. Aside from the bruise on her cheek, she looked strong—strong enough that she didn't want or need his help.

He opened the door for her that led into the shop. An elderly man stood behind the counter, sipping on a cup of coffee.

"Hi. Let me know if I can help you with anything," the man said with a slight Canadian accent.

"Thanks. Actually, I was hoping to ask you a few questions." Casper reached into his back pocket, pulling out his wallet to flash his badge. "We found some evidence linking a person to this store. We're just hoping to get any information you may have that can help us."

The man ran his hand over his gray hair, which sat in a plastered comb-over across his balding dome. "I...sure. I guess."

Casper pulled up the picture of the receipt on his phone. "We found this. According to the date, it's from a couple of days ago. Is there anything you can tell me about it?" He set his phone down on the counter so the man could take a look.

"Sure..." The man squinted as he leaned in and studied the details. "Hmm, I was working that day, but you know, we get so many people in and out of these doors throughout the season that it's hard to keep track from one day to the next."

"It's important that you remember." He glanced around, looking for some type of security cameras, but there were none in sight. "Do you have any cameras, anything we could look at, anything that could jog your memory?"

Lex stepped closer to the counter and motioned toward the picture on his phone. "What kind of thing would you have sold for that amount?"

The guy looked around the store. "With this cold weather we've been selling a lot of sweatshirts." His face brightened. "Actually, there was a lady who came in that day. Bought a sweatshirt and a Coke. With tax, that puts us right around that amount." He zoomed in on the time.

A woman? Was it possible the green bag hadn't belonged to the man they'd found disarticulated in the timber?

"Let me check my sales." He turned to his computer and tapped away at the keys.

Casper nodded appreciatively at Lex. Of course the man behind the counter wouldn't think in terms of people. Rather, he'd think in terms of the merchandise that had moved.

"Yeah," the man said with a nod. "Here it is." He tilted the screen so they could see his copy of the transaction. "She paid with cash. American. Wasn't very talkative." He pointed toward a rack of blue sweatshirts. "She bought a plain blue sweatshirt, just a small logo of the park on the breast."

"Can you describe the woman?"

The man looked up and squinted, like he could pull the woman's image from thin air. "I don't remember much about her. She was in her midthirties. Had darkish hair?" His tone didn't incite a tremendous amount of confidence.

"You remember what she was wearing?"

The guy nodded. "Oh yeah, that was the weird thing. She was wearing a leather vest thing. Had some patches."

"You mean the woman was part of a motorcycle club?" Lex asked, excited.

The man looked at Lex and shrugged. "I guess. I think she was driving a motorcycle or something. Oh, and she didn't want a plastic bag—which is just fine if you ask me. It might only save me a few cents, but it adds up, you know."

"Why didn't she want a bag?" Casper asked.

"If I remember right, she put the sweatshirt on. And she stuck the Coke in her backpack."

Casper twitched. "By chance, do you remember what her backpack looked like?"

"It was green. Kind of a military-style one."

"Did you get a good look at her leather vest?" Lex asked.

The man tapped on the counter. "I didn't get a real good look. But I think there was a set of green wings and there was a badge thingy that read "Property." He motioned toward the place on his chest, right above his right pec where it would have been.

"A top rocker. Did it have any kind of name underneath?"

"Couldn't tell ya." The guy shrugged.

"Is there anything else you can tell us? Anything at all?" Lex pressed.

"I'm sorry..." The guy shook his head. "But

if you have any more questions, you can come around anytime."

They may not have found the identity of their victim, but with the man's help, they'd found their break, a lead that could help Casper save face. And maybe it could keep him from losing another job—or at least let him keep it for a little longer.

Heck, if things went right, he could stick around. If he did, maybe he could give falling in love another shot. Then again, love was far more dangerous than the people he chased.

Chapter Six

The wind blew cold against Lex's skin as she walked out of the shop. Casper's face was pulled tight into a worried expression, one she had come to know so well at the hospital. His grin was much more handsome, but even serious he was so good-looking that he made her uncomfortable.

She sucked in a breath as the icy-fingered breeze brushed over her skin and made goose bumps rise on her arms.

He glanced over at her, and his face grew impossibly tighter. "Are you okay? Do you need to sit down? Damn it. I knew I shouldn't have brought you up here."

Her chill was quickly replaced by annoyance. "First, I'm fine, just cold—you don't need to get worked up over me. I'm a big girl. If I didn't think I should be out here I wouldn't be. I know my limits." She held up her fingers. "And second, do you think this is just *your* investigation? In every way this is my jurisdiction. Your boss called in a favor in asking to include you on the body's recovery and subsequent investigation."

Casper's face fell. "You talked to Randall?"

"He explained that the CBP wanted to be included on this as it involved a potential illegal incident that may blow back on your post."

His cheeks paled. "I didn't let this guy through. Anything suspicious and I'm on top of it."

"You better hope that's the case." She felt sorry for him as she watched what little color was left in his face drain away. "Your boss sounded none too pleased that you had let an undocumented through—I can only imagine what he's thinking if he heard about the drugs."

"I never saw a guy carrying a military-style bag come through—I would have noticed," he said, an edge of panic and fear in his voice. "There's no way I'm responsible for what is happening here— heck, he might not have ever crossed the border, or he may have slipped it. Thousands of people just walk over the border near my post. I can't investigate every sensor that goes off—in fact, Randall wouldn't even allow me to investigate ten percent of them. The only reason he let me this time is in case the press got ahold of this…"

"Don't worry, Casper, we'll figure this out. In

fact, we're going to do such a good job buttoning this up that you or I may be the next employee of the month." She tried to take the edge off, but she couldn't manage the inflection needed in her voice to sell it, and the joke fell flat.

He quirked an eyebrow as he looked at her. "Somehow I find you getting employee of the month hard to believe. You… You are too independent. Does your boss even know where you are?"

Was he really going to pick a fight? With Travis she normally would have stepped right up to the plate, taken a swing and let the fight commence, but with Casper it was different. He wasn't picking a fight out of a need for control; it felt as if it was more out of the need to protect.

As a former FBI agent it made sense that he would have the intrinsic need to safeguard those around him. Yet that still didn't answer why he'd been sent to the nowhere border. And as badly as she wanted to get the real answer, with them halfway to a fight it didn't seem like the right time to try and pry it out of him.

She sighed in an attempt to compose herself. "I think you're confusing independent with determined. And right now, Casper, I think determination is going to be the only thing that is going to solve this case. Then I can check in with my boss."

As she spoke, her phone stirred to life and

belted the song "Born to be Wild." Heat rushed to her cheeks as she thought of how much it paralleled the conversation they were having, and she turned away in order to avoid any sort of self-righteous smirk that was probably playing across Casper's lips.

"Alexis?" She was met with her boss Head Ranger Denver Dragger's voice. "Where are you?"

Speak of the devil.

She caught a glimpse of Casper in the window, complete with that damned smirk.

"Uh…what?" She tried to force herself to concentrate on her boss's voice, but she couldn't stop looking at Casper's wide-set jaw and the stubble that riddled his cheeks. He needed a shave, but something about the scruffy look made a part of her stir to life.

The head ranger coughed. "Alexis, are you listening?"

"Yeah. I'm here. We're just tracking down a lead on the dead hiker case—I think we're close to getting an ID on him, and maybe we can figure out where the drugs were coming from and where he was taking them."

She could almost hear Dragger shake his head. "Lex, I'm calling because I wanted to check on you after your little accident, but if I'd known you were going to use your day off to go traipsing around the world…" He paused. "There's work that needs to be done. As it is, if you're feeling better, I need you to come to work in the morning. I want someone else on this. I need you at the Sperry Chalet. It needs to be buttoned up for the season."

The Sperry Chalet was a primitive cabin only accessible by horse or hike. Normally she liked to help with the winterization process, but this time it didn't call to her like the investigation. She certainly couldn't hand it over to someone else now, when they were so close to finding some kind of answers. "Sir, I'm afraid I'm—"

"If you're not in your bed right now, then I fully expect to see you at the station in the morning." He hung up without waiting for her response.

Normally she and Dragger saw eye to eye on most things and they treated each other with a sort of mutual respect. In fact, he'd once made a point of telling her that she shouldn't look at him like a boss, rather as a comrade in arms. They had always been friends—at least up to now.

Maybe she had simply misunderstood the man. Or perhaps it was that things were winding down for the season and he was just stressing about everything that needed to be checked off the list. God knew there was a boatload of things that needed to be done; cabins that needed to be winterized, chalets that needed to be locked down and prepared for the onslaught of snow that they would undoubtedly receive, and there were the ongoing needs of the thousands of guests that ventured through their park via roads and trails. Truth be told, they were sorely understaffed and underfunded, but that hadn't ever caused a rift in their friendship before. She just couldn't understand why it would suddenly drive a wedge between them—and she certainly didn't understand why he would want her to hand off the investigation.

This was hardly her first investigation into a death in the park. Every summer a few more people found their ends there. Last summer she and Travis had handled an investigation into a woman who had fallen into McDonald Creek and drowned. After they'd concluded their investigation, Dragger had made a point of commending them.

He liked her work, so why was he pulling her?

She wasn't going to change his mind. Not Dragger's.

She dropped the phone back into her pocket. She'd only have a few more hours until tomorrow morning, and then this case would fall into someone else's hands.

"What's going on?"

She looked up at Casper and their eyes locked. "It looks like I called it down on myself, and my independence just bit me in the ass." Her heart sank as she looked at him. "I'm supposed to go to work on the seasonal projects tomorrow, and this investigation will be taken over by another ranger. You're right, I don't think I'll be getting employee of the month after all."

"If that's the case, we're going to need to work fast. Who's Sherlock without his Watson?"

"You are really calling yourself Sherlock?" Her spirits picked up.

He nodded, straightening his back and pretending to hold a pipe.

At least the man knew how to make her smile. "I should be Sherlock," she said with a laugh. "Regardless, where would you like to begin, my dear man?" she asked in her worst British accent.

His laugh rippled through the air and spread through the quiet street.

A man sitting alone on a park bench turned and looked at them and gave them an appreciative nod.

"Shhh…" She reached over and touched Casper's arm as she giggled. His skin was hot and penetrating on her cold fingers and she drew them back.

He looked to the place where she had touched him. "This could be simple. The man in the shop told us that it's a woman and she was wearing a cut. That may mean she is a part of a local motorcycle club. The Hells Keepers are in control of the territory, all the way out to Washington as far as I know."

"Could she have just been a leisure rider?" They were up through the park all the time, weekend bikers. Often they could be found at the top of Logan's Pass, victims of the stalling effects of the elevation.

"A leisure rider doesn't wear a cut, especially not one with a property top rocker and a-wings patch."

"Is that supposed to mean something to me?"

"Women aren't welcomed into the motorcycle clubs, or the one-percenters—the outlaws. Their only way in is by being a turnabout, a Mama, or they can be one of the guys' old ladies."

"Old lady?"

"A woman that's in a serious relationship with one of the men. They don't have to do anything like the turnabouts—selling their body or being a thing that is passed around the club—but even old ladies have to do the men's bidding."

"That makes absolutely no sense to me. What kind of woman would want to be used like that? Or worse, to let their man control every aspect of their lives?"

"I get why you wouldn't understand, Ms. Independent, but there are a lot of women out there who are nothing like you. They like to have the safety net that an outlaw club provides. Sure, they run outside of the rules of social customs, but that kind of life brings danger. In exchange for protection they respect and trust those in their club—it's their family."

She gave him a confused look.

"Their strength lies in the power of the brotherhood, and the women who go out of the way to protect them. The ATF, you know the Bureau of Alcohol, Tobacco, Firearms and Explosives, and other federal agencies are constantly trying to infiltrate their group."

"Because of fear of the power they have?"

Casper took her gently by the hand and helped her back into the car. "They are more powerful than most average citizens realize. These groups, and those like them, are some of the biggest smugglers of drugs and weapons into the United States, and they have well-developed and successful distribution channels."

"Haven't the agencies taken them down? I see the things on TV all the time, where one of you Feds goes undercover and infiltrates their group and brings them to their knees." She buckled her seat belt as Casper walked around, got in and started the car.

He took off his hat and slid it onto the seat between them like it was a physical reminder that they needed to be kept apart. "The government has had some big busts in the past, but truth be told, nailing these guys is a bit like playing Whack-a-Mole. You knock one chapter down only to have another one spring up near them and take over the business they left behind. There's always someone who wants to live outside the norms that society has placed on them—and they use their fringe lifestyle to build a network of those just like them."

"A 'divided they stand' kind of thing?" she asked.

"Exactly. Even for the women."

In a way she could understand a woman's desire to want to be loved, to be part of a group, and find acceptance—especially when the world was against her. Heck, she could definitely understand the world being against her. Ever since she was a child and she had been in the foster system and then shuffled from one house to the next, she had known the fear of being alone and the feelings of powerlessness that followed on its heels. Maybe she wasn't so different from the women after all. Maybe the only difference was in the fact that now she was fighting violence while they were simply fighting the world.

He drove down the shop-lined road that led to a park on the edge of town near the Prince of Wales

Hotel. Passing the palatial expanse of green lawns and rows of white and pink roses that adorned the lawn of the hotel, they entered the forest. Large pines poked their heads up from the crowd, each one struggling for a little more sunlight than the one next to it.

"Where are we going?" she asked.

"The trailhead." He dipped his chin, motioning down the road. "It may be a long shot, but maybe we can find something there. The woman has to be involved somehow with the guy and his drugs. If they were coming from the store, then this trailhead seems to be the most likely place where our vic would have started his hike.

"You know what? I bet you money that this guy came through after my checkpoint closed. It makes sense. The time on the receipt was six p.m. From the trailhead it was about a three-hour hike. The guy must have planned this whole thing to avoid getting caught." As he spoke, his eyes brightened and color rose in his face.

He turned and the sunshine glistened off his chestnut-colored hair, making it sparkle, and there was a hat ring where his hat hugged his head. He caught her staring and sent her that sexy grin that sometimes drove her crazy, but right now she wouldn't change it for the world. As he looked at her in that moment, it was as if he was peering down into the very core of her and seeing her for the woman she truly was. The thought made her shift in her seat and she glanced away.

She didn't want him to look at her like that. She would hate for him to look into her soul and not like what he saw. She'd already had far too much rejection in her life.

Everyone had baggage, and though he knew about Travis and the divorce, he didn't need to know any more about her—or about her past. Some things were just better left unknown.

The road came to an end, looping around, and it was edged with parking spots. Casper pulled to a stop and got out. He picked up his hat from the seat and shoved it on his head, hiding his beautiful hair.

The parking lot had a few cars, most with Montana or Alberta plates, but there wasn't a motorcycle in sight.

"What do you think we should be looking for exactly?"

"Most of the time when it comes down to investigating a crime, there's a few things you generally look for—but in this case, all I can say is that I hope that we'll know what we're looking for when we see it," Casper said.

She hoped he was right. They didn't have much time and she'd hate to waste what little they had on an idea that wouldn't pan out.

Casper walked around the asphalt parking lot, picking his way one spot at a time, looking at the tire tracks like they held some kind of clue. Yet after about the tenth parking space, he ran his hand over the brim of his hat in frustration. "Damn it, I was hoping we'd get lucky."

"It's fine. There has to be something else we can find. Maybe we can get someone else to give us a lead on the girl. Maybe someone saw her coming out of the shop, or meeting up with the man whose body we found." She touched his arm, trying to reassure him, but the same familiar burn returned and she dropped her hand.

Would it be that way every time she touched him?

"Let's just keep looking. Maybe peek over there in the tree line," she said, motioning toward the woods.

She looked down at her fingers and wiggled them as he walked away; maybe she was just imagining the feeling when she'd touched him. Maybe it wasn't real.

She thought back to the first time she had ever come to Glacier National Park. She had been young, and it hadn't been long after she had been moved into her third foster home when her foster mother, Melody Finch, had brought her to Lake McDonald. The waters were so clear that the colored stones made it look like a rainbow had been trapped under the weight of the water. The peaks of the mountains had been covered in thick layers of snow, framing the natural beauty that surrounded her.

For the first time in her life, she had felt truly and absolutely free. In that moment, with Melody holding her hand, she had felt the burn—the love of the place that surrounded her and the love for the woman who could show her such beauty and kindness.

Looking back, she realized the sacrifice her adoptive mother had made in taking her, a child who had been through so much, into her home. She'd loved her and raised her as her own, never treating her differently than Paul, or her sisters Raquel, Treana or Anna. Without her adoptive mother, Lex didn't doubt for a second that she would have become a lost soul—perhaps just like the biker woman they were tracking.

It was strange how one moment in time, one little feeling, could change a life forever.

She glanced over at Casper. He was working his way through a thick stand of timber at the side of the parking lot. Though it wasn't especially warm, there was the sheen of sweat on his face.

"Come here," he said, motioning toward her.

She gingerly made her way through the gnarled

and ripping fingers of the pines to his side. On the ground, at the tip of his cowboy boot, was a thin trail, almost like a game trail, but the ground was black with organic matter that had been torn away rather than worn down.

"Someone's been driving through here," he said, pointing his chin in the direction the trail headed.

The trees that surrounded them were too close and too thick for a normal vehicle to fit through. On the other hand, it would have perfectly fit a motorcycle.

Casper followed the path into the woods.

"Wait," she called after him, hurrying to catch up. She took hold of his arm and gently tugged him to a stop. "Wait. What if this is some kind of trap?" The trail ahead of them was swallowed up by the shadows of the trees, silently disappearing into the foreboding forest.

Her question didn't seem unreasonable; any number of things could have been waiting for them at the end of the path, but Casper looked at her like she was a skittish deer.

"Don't worry, there's probably nothing on this thing. I just need to take a look," he said, his voice soft and low. She wasn't a damned deer. She wasn't weak—at least, she wouldn't ever be again. She'd had too much of that as a child. Her strength was the only thing that would keep her sane.

"Maybe it was just some kids having a good time with their dirt bikes, Lex. Trust me, you don't have to be scared. I'd never let someone hurt you."

Casper reached down and took her hand. His fingers were rough with calluses and his skin was hot, and the burn deep down in her core returned. The movement came so fast and unexpectedly, that before she could stop herself, she wrapped her fingers around his. He led her forward, and her apprehension decreased with each step they took together.

Though she was supposed to be watching for clues, all she could look at was their entwined fingers. She knew it was her hand in his, but she couldn't feel where she ended and he began; rather, it was as if they were one, tightening and loosening as they flexed and moved.

Her breath hitched in her throat as she imagined what it would be like to feel him in another, more intimate way. Her cheeks warmed and she forced herself to look away from his thick, work-worn fingers.

She closed her eyes and tried to collect her breath and force her thoughts away from the forbidden embers of dreams that he stoked.

Not watching, she took a step forward, colliding with him, and let go. "Whoa, I'm sorry," she said, afraid that if she looked into his eyes again, he might be able to catch a glimpse of her thoughts and the lurid dreams that she was struggling to hide.

He didn't say anything, and she glanced up. His back was turned to her, and he was looking at something she couldn't see. She stepped around him in hopes of seeing what had caught his attention.

There, parked at the base of a tree and poorly concealed by a smattering of broken-off pine boughs, was a Harley-Davidson. A thin layer of dust covered the bike's leather seat and several days' worth of fallen pine needles were littered over its body.

Casper had been right. Sometimes you knew a clue the moment you saw it; and this one had two giant skulls painted on the bike's gas tank that stared right back.

Chapter Seven

The two skulls leaned against each other like they had been set there as part of some kind of Mayan sacrifice to the gods, except the sockets were painted in a red so deep that it reminded him of the color of spent arterial blood. At the base of the skulls was a coiled snake, its diamond-shaped head sitting between them, as if waiting for the exact moment to deliver the fatal blow.

The rear fender was midnight-black, like the base coat on the gas tank, but instead of skulls it had strands of silver razor wire running down its length.

"This thing just needs a danger sign and I think it would be the full package," Lex joked.

He chuckled. "Everything about it just screams *hug me*, doesn't it?"

He motioned toward the Madness and Mayhem motto that was etched into the gas tank's lid and nodded. "I think you nailed it. I mean, just look. He must be a big softy."

"There's no license plate," she said, pointing to two empty screw holes where someone had deliberately removed the plate. "So, how can we find the owner?"

"There should be a VIN." He searched the bike's frame, but he was surprised when there was nothing more than a series of scratches where someone had scoured away the machine's identification numbers. This was a bike of someone who knew there was a possibility of leaving it behind—and didn't want it to be traced back to the owner.

Casper searched the ground around the bike, but there was nothing, not even a cigarette butt. Whoever had dumped the thing had been clean— too clean. It made his skin prickle.

Even so, they must not have understood the tenacity of a CBP agent on a mission; especially when the more time that went by, the less likely they were to find out the identity of the man who had been running drugs. If they couldn't identify the man quickly, there was no chance they would find the person supplying the Canadian Blue and put a stop to the influx of drugs, at least through Casper's territory.

"Did you find it?" Lex asked.

"It's not there." He kicked the dirt near the back tire as he stood up.

"Is there another way?"

"With no plate and no VIN, there's only one other way we can try and find out who this bike belonged to—we're going to have to go to street level."

"What do you mean?"

He smiled. "I got a friend in the US Marshal Service, Evan Steel—he can put some feelers out in the biker community and the prison system. Maybe he can get a lead on this guy for us. Then we can track down the woman from the store. In the meantime, unfortunately, we're going to have to call in the locals on this one. We're on the wrong side of the border."

He made a quick call to the local Mounties to report an abandoned vehicle and the possibility of its tie into a criminal investigation.

"They're on their way," he said, slipping the phone back into the breast pocket of his blue flannel button-up shirt. As he spoke, the sky above them darkened, sending ominous, skeletal shadows. "They said they'd be here in about an hour. From the looks of things, we may be waiting out here in the rain."

A rattle of thunder echoed through the timber, the sound deep and crashing and so loud that Lex jumped. Casper had a primal urge to reach over and pull her into his arms and shelter her from the storm, but he held back.

"Do you want to go back to the truck, wait there?" Lex asked, jabbing her thumb in the direction of the parking lot.

Her eyes were wide with fear, and the urge in him worsened. Here was this strong, incredible woman…a woman who could handle death and car accidents like they were just another day at the park, yet she was afraid of thunder. The thought was endearing.

Lex stepped beside him and took his hand. He squeezed her and let their entwined hands fall between them as he slowly led the way back down the trail toward the car. He took his time picking through the timber and weaving around trees in an attempt to keep holding her—it felt so good, her skin against his.

His shoulder brushed hers and as they touched, he could have sworn he heard her breath catch, but he told himself that it was nothing more than the sound of the wind in the trees.

Rain spattered down, kicking up the thick black dirt at their feet and splashing mud against their legs as they walked. Lex was frowning as if she realized that Casper was intentionally lengthening their hike, but she said nothing and instead gripped him tighter.

He led her toward a stand of trees where two could barely fit side by side and, as they moved, she was forced to turn slightly, putting them face-to-face. She blinked slowly as she looked up at him.

The rain fell around them, wetting their faces like spent tears.

Reaching up, he cupped her face in his hands, running his thumbs over the soft skin of her bottom lip. Her warm breath caressed his finger, a hard contrast against the cold rain, and the feeling only made him want her more.

"You're so damned beautiful." He moved closer, so close he could feel the warmth radiating off her body.

She stepped forward, not waiting for him to make the first move, and pressed her lips to his. She ran her tongue against his, making a need deep inside him move with carnal hunger. He wanted her. This. Now.

He pulled her against him; her body was soft and supplicating as he pressed her to the bark of the tree. He trailed his fingers down her back, grazing over the intersection of her lower back and the top of her pants and cupping her. She was round in his hands, strong and muscular and even better than he could have imagined.

Squeezing her gently, she moaned softly into his mouth, making him rise with a want so urgent that he felt the urge to growl. There was something so right about this moment and this woman that, as he held her, all of his misgivings slipped away. Maybe they could make something work out. He'd be reassigned to another point of entry over the winter, but he could stay close—anything to be near her.

The tree bark crackled as he lifted her and wrapped her legs around his waist. She was hot against him—her body's response to their kiss. She wanted this. She wanted him.

Breaking their bond, she leaned her head back and sucked in a breath as he trailed kisses down her neck. He pulled back her shirt, just exposing the top of her pale skin. She was so soft. So warm. So his.

"Is that you, eh?" a man with a thick Canadian accent asked, shattering the moment.

Casper let go of her, and she swayed slightly. He took her hand in an attempt to help her catch her balance, but truth be told, he was unsteady, as well.

He turned at the sound of a man's laugh.

"We didn't mean to interrupt you all. If you want we can all come back a little later—give you some privacy, you know."

He wanted them to disappear, so he and Lex could finish what they had started. But before he could speak, Lex, who was brushing off the back of her shirt, stepped around him. "We were just waiting for you. Glad to see you could finally make it."

Casper gave the sergeant and his man a quick rundown of the case, giving them what little information he had. It ate at him to include more people in the investigation, but it was good to have their cooperation in finding anything on their side of the border.

The sergeant nodded as he spoke, but the man couldn't seem to keep his gaze from drifting to the bike.

"You know anything about the bike? Who it may belong to?" Casper asked.

The officer beside the sergeant leaned in and whispered something about a razor, but as hard as he tried, Casper couldn't hear everything that was said.

The sergeant shook his head and gave the man a look that said shut up in every language. The man shut his mouth immediately.

"I'm afraid we haven't a clue, but rest assured we will be looking into this bike and its owner," the sergeant said.

"We'd appreciate it. Any information we could get would be great. Right now we have little more to go on than a wing and a prayer," Casper said in an attempt to build a little comraderie.

The sergeant smiled; the motion was so tight and high that Casper suspected the man liked to hear about their failings.

Did they think they were better than some silly Americans? Or was it something else that made the man react like he had?

He shook the thoughts from his head. In the end, it didn't matter what the Mounties thought. They just needed to work together to get as much information as possible.

As they loaded the bike onto the flatbed truck to tow it away, Casper made sure to snap a few more close-ups of the bike and scene. He emailed them with a note explaining everything to his friend, Evan Steel.

His phone rang. He turned to Lex. "Will you be okay here?"

She gave him a confused look. "Why wouldn't I be?"

He glanced over at the Mounties, who were busy talking to the tow truck driver. Maybe he had them all wrong, but a gut feeling warned him not to leave them alone with Lex. "I gotta answer this, but stay where I can see you, okay?"

She frowned and gave him a confused grin that he found so sexy. "No problem."

He walked back into the timber and out of earshot from the Mounties, but close enough that he could still keep an eye on Lex.

"Stuck, huh?" Steel said, his words resting in the middle ground between a question and a statement.

"Never said that," Casper said with an acknowledging chuckle. "But I'm glad you called. You ever seen a bike like this one before?"

"I had a chance to run an image search for you in the database. According to what I found, the two skulls and the snake image is used by only one specific motorcycle club, a group called Hells Keepers. It sounds like they do a lot of the club's dirty business."

"Where are they out of?"

"Their main clubhouse is in Calgary, but there are quite a few chapters along the borders."

"You know anybody that has had run-ins with these guys?"

Steel sighed. "They are slippery. From what I've managed to put together about them, they are just like American clubs—they have their own laws, and when we run into them, we have a heck of a time trying to pull any information. They are one-percenters through and through."

"Do you know if they are missing a member? We'd like to get an ID on the body."

Steel's laughter was as tough-sounding as his name. "Trying to find out if there is a missing member would be like trying to find out if ghosts are real—in all honesty, that's basically what these people are. They have nearly perfected a lifestyle out of staying off law enforcement's radar, and when and if they are in it, they know how to disappear."

"Do you think you can at least get me a list of the most recent known members?"

"I'll send you whatever I can get my hands on."

Casper glanced over at Lex, who was leaning against their car. She was staring off into the distance and he wondered what she was thinking. Absentmindedly, she ran her finger slowly over her lip and his body went rigid with the thought of their kiss.

"Do you know anything about their women?"

"That we have a little more information on— we have a few of their names and addresses. I'll send you that, as well."

"Great, thanks."

"And hey, Lawrence, if you need anything else, don't hesitate. I've made it a personal mission of mine to bring down as many of these clubs as possible. They're bad business… They're one of the abhorrent parts of our society. I hope you get your bastards. And who knows, maybe we can use this to help raise awareness of drug running across the Canadian border? Everyone talks about Mexico, but Canadian suppliers are just as dangerous and their drugs are more diversified."

Casper moved to hang up but stopped. "Steel, have you seen any new Canadian Blue hitting the streets in and around Montana?"

"Over the last few years, the DEA has seen a steady stream of Blue coming through Montana and spreading across the Dakotas, Idaho and Washington."

Casper snorted. "I don't know for sure, but if I had to bet, all of it is being run through the park."

Steel remained silent, almost as if he was digesting the information. "If that's true," he finally said, "then you need to do everything in your power to get to the bottom of this."

"Thanks, Steel. 'Preciate your time." Casper walked toward Lex.

"Lawrence, let me give you one more little piece of advice. These guys you're investigating… they're bad dudes. In the last year, we've heard whispers of their involvement in some revolting crimes—crimes involving women and children, even animals. These men have their own sense of right and wrong and what they consider justice. You need to be careful. They'll stop at nothing to keep themselves out of the public eye—even if that means taking out a federal officer or his family and friends."

He slipped his fingers into Lex's. Her hands were cold and she wrapped her free hand around her body in an attempt to warm herself.

There was no way he'd let these bastards get their hands on the only person he cared about.

"Thanks for the heads-up, Steel."

"Like I said, Lawrence, best of luck. Keep your head out of the sights."

Steel hung up, and as the phone clicked, chills ran down Casper's spine. It wasn't his head that he was worried about.

He made his way over to the tow truck where the Mounties were standing around, chatting about the case. The sergeant was talking with his hands, making some point that Casper couldn't quite hear.

"You guys ever heard of Hells Keepers?" he said, interrupting them.

The sergeant stopped and slowly turned. "What about 'em?"

"So you know who they are?" Casper pressed.

"Sure, we know. You think this is one of theirs?" He pointed toward the bike that was strapped to the flatbed and his gaze flickered to another of the officers as though he was hoping for a witness, making Casper's internal danger meter spike.

What did this Mountie know about the club?

When Casper had mentioned the club's name it was as if the air had charged around them and they were one spark away from an explosion. The last thing he needed was the motorcycle club finding out that they were a part of an investigation. Steel had made a point of telling him to stay out of their sightline.

"We're not sure," he said, careful to avoid the full truth, but it was a fine line between getting the information they needed and raising flags. "We're thinking it's probably not related to the club," he lied. "By chance, though, you heard of any of them who've had problems lately?"

"Look, if you think this has anything to do with the Keepers, I would strongly recommend that you look elsewhere. Bad things happen to people who stick their noses in places they don't belong, eh?" He looked over at Lex.

Every hair on his arms stood straight at the poorly veiled threat. He didn't know how the man was involved with the club, or if he was, but he couldn't put Lex at risk.

"We'll drop it. No problem. I was just wondering—that's all. The thought stops here."

The man visibly relaxed and he leaned against the flatbed. "Anybody ever tell you that you're a smart man? If you were a Canadian, we'd hire you."

He couldn't even fake a smile. "I'll keep that in mind." As he spoke, the bitter taste of bile rose from his stomach. He'd screwed up in his past. He'd made his fair share of mistakes. But unlike the men who stood in front of him, he'd never be crooked.

Chapter Eight

As they made the long drive back toward her cabin, Lex checked her phone. They finally hit an area with service after they came over the border and back into Montana.

"Stop," she said with a wave of her hand. "I got service."

Casper pulled the car over to the side of the road. In the distance were the snowcapped mountains of the park.

She typed her query into the search engine: *Hells Keepers + crimes.*

The pages popped up with headlines from the local newspapers. Most of the headlines were about murders and thefts, and a few talked about drug deals gone bad. They had found themselves deep in a world of crime.

"Holy cow," she said in a single long breath. "Do you know who these Keeper guys are?"

Casper's hands tightened on the steering wheel, almost like he knew exactly who they were but had been too afraid to tell her.

"What's going on, Casper?" she asked, dropping her phone into her lap.

"Nothing," he said, but his eyes were dark.

"Don't lie to me. What's wrong?"

He glanced over at her and, taking off his hat, set it on the dashboard. He ran his hands over his face and through his hair in exasperation. "I'm fine... I just think it's going to be better if you get away from all this—this investigation."

"What did I do?" she asked, trying to stop the hurt from leaking out into her voice.

All she had been trying to do for the last two days was solve this so they both could get their jobs done. Now, after a strange meeting with the Royal Canadian Mounties, she was on the outs. It didn't make sense.

"You didn't do anything, Lex. I promise." He sighed, but the sound only made her angrier and more hurt.

Was he tired of her?

She tried to remind herself they were only friends and maybe barely that. Sure, they had shared the kiss in the woods, but ever since they had gotten caught he had barely been able to look at her.

"Is this because of what happened…you know, back there?" She motioned in the direction they'd come from, but she was sure he knew exactly what she was talking about.

"Huh?"

She gnashed her teeth, but tried to control her anger. "You know. The kiss. Whatever it was back there. Did I do something wrong?"

He guppied, his mouth making tight "O" shapes while he searched for words.

"I agree. What happened back there—it was a mistake," she continued. "Won't happen again."

"Lex, no. That's not it. It's just that—"

"Just drop it. Let's both agree we can't make that kind of mistake again. We are both better off if we just get back to what we're good at." She thought about jumping out of the car and getting away from the tense air that simmered between them, but there was nowhere to go. They were miles away from the nearest town, which was no larger than a bar and a church. And even if she made it to one of those little rinky-dink towns, she still would need to make it home. There was no running away from this.

"Lex, I…that wasn't a mistake. I wanted that. I wanted you."

"You don't need to try to make me feel better. It

was a stupid thing to do. What were we thinking? Tomorrow I have to go back to my regular job, and next week I will be in Apgar watching the winter snowshoers. You'll be… Where will you be? Do you even know? I mean, look, you don't tell me anything. Anytime I ask you anything real about yourself you repel from me like I'm asking you about your deepest, darkest secrets. I don't even know who you really are."

He leaned toward her and moved to take her hands, but she pulled back. "No, Casper. Don't touch me."

It was almost as if her words were a branding iron. He recoiled and his face was filled with pain. Maybe she had been wrong in coming at him as she had, but she wasn't wrong in her thinking. He hadn't been open with her, and if he couldn't be open he wasn't someone she wanted in her life.

She thought back to Travis. So much of their time together had been shrouded in secrets—late nights, unanswered phone calls and lies. He'd been cruel to her, telling her that she lived in a world built on unrealistic expectations when she asked him where he'd been or what he'd been doing. He'd never cheated on her—as far as she knew—but things between them had always been strained; that was, until she had started to pull away. It was strange how a man never wanted you too close until you were ready to walk out the door.

She never wanted to be treated like that again—not by any man, not even the handsome cowboy she had started to care about over the last few days. No matter what, she had to be careful, her heart was too fragile to be given to the wrong man.

"What do you want to know?" Casper finally asked, but there was still the same pained expression on his face.

"I don't want to have to force you into telling me anything. If you want me like you say you do, then you should *want* to talk to me. You should want to tell me your secrets—your past."

"It isn't that easy, Lex."

"If you care about me, then it *is* that easy."

"Damn it, Lex… I'm not like you. I haven't had an easy go of things over the last few years. My life has turned to complete crap. I lost the only job I cared about and now I'm stuck up here—at the most desolate place in the contiguous United States."

She prickled with anger. "You think I've had it easy, Casper? You think my life has been nothing but hiking and wildflowers?"

"You know what?" Casper rebuked. "You've accused me of not telling you anything, but has it occurred to you that you haven't told me anything, either? What happened between you and Travis?"

Fury roiled in her gut at the sound of Travis's name. "Do you really care?"

Casper's face softened. "No matter what you think, I do. Maybe we can't have a relationship—since that's not what you want—but at least maybe we can be friends."

A whisper of guilt filled her; his past caused him pain—he'd made that clear by attacking her and Travis's relationship—but that didn't mean that his past hadn't happened or that she could be kept in the dark. Yet she couldn't help the feeling that crept through her that told her if she kept pushing, the only thing she would achieve was making each of them more frustrated.

If he wanted this, he would talk to her. Until then, she couldn't risk her heart.

"Sure," she said. "Friends."

He seemed satisfied, like they had solved the problems that rested between them. Didn't he understand that she wanted him to fight for her—even if that battle was in himself? If he was the man she wanted, he would figure it out—if not, then things weren't meant to be. As much as she was attracted to him, as badly as she wanted to feel his kiss and fall into his arms again, she couldn't force a relationship to happen.

She clicked on her phone and stared down at the screen in an attempt to squelch her feelings.

"What did you find?" he asked, clearly oblivious of the turmoil inside her.

"These guys, these Keeper dudes, have an ongoing battle happening with the Canadian Parliament. There's a piece here about one of them being charged with attempted murder after he went after one of the local senators." She lifted the phone for him to see. "According to the article, the Keeper was only sentenced to three years in prison even though he managed to get a shot off on the Senator, hitting him once in the leg."

"Really?" Casper reached over and took the phone from her, his fingers grazing hers.

The touch made a surge of attraction pulse through her, but she pushed the feelings aside. No matter what her body told her, she needed to focus on the investigation.

"Look at Gabrielle Giffords," Casper continued. "The shooter, the Loughner guy, got seven consecutive life terms in a federal prison. You can't tell me that the Canadian government would just let some guy off with a slap on the wrist for something like that."

"But that's exactly what they did."

Casper stared out the window. "That just doesn't make sense... Something has to be wrong. The media would have used this shooter and what he attempted to do as propaganda to stop something like that from happening again. Why would the justice system have just let him off?"

"What if he was meant to take a fall?"

Casper looked over at her. "You could be right. Or he was so deep into underworld politics that they were afraid of him. Somewhere there has to be something that explains it."

He tapped on the screen, moving through the article.

"From this, it looks like the guy's legal name is Peter Kagger, but went by 'Bug-Eye.' He's currently sitting in a Canadian prison."

She leaned close to Casper, so close that she could smell the rain and fresh air on his skin, a scent as intoxicating as his touch. She closed her eyes and took it deep into her lungs, pulling him into her like the simple action of growing closer could fix all of their problems.

On her phone's screen a picture caught her eye. There was a man wearing a black leather vest with patches sewn over it, who she assumed was the biker Peter Kagger, and standing next to him was a woman. Her eyes were tired and her face was taut and gaunt, merely skin stretched over bone. She looked like she had been to hell and back.

"Who's that woman?"

He enlarged the picture, making the woman look even more skeletal now that she filled the screen. Her eyes were dark and filled with what looked like even darker secrets.

"From the caption," Casper said, "it looks like her name is Lois Trainer. They said she was a friend of Kagger's. There's no mention of her in the article."

"Wait a minute," Alexis said, sitting back. "What do you think the connection may be?"

"I know Kagger isn't the guy in the woods, but with what few pieces we have to work with, I think looking into this is as good a place as any to start. If we can find this Lois Trainer, maybe she can give us a clue about anyone who has gone missing from the club." His eyes widened and his mouth moved as if he had just remembered something. "Wait, Steel said he was going to send me a list of the women associated with the MC that the FBI has been tracking. Maybe we can pull something from that."

He handed her phone back to her and took out his to check his email. It was hot in her hands where he had been holding on to it. He had such passion for his work. No wonder he hadn't wanted to talk about losing his last position—the job he truly wanted. He was a man whose self-worth was built through his work—or wherever his passion lay. And, no doubt, when his work had been stripped away, he'd lost a part of himself.

As she looked at him, at the fine lines that were nestled around his gorgeous caramel-colored eyes, her anger at his inability to open up somewhat dissipated—though it didn't disappear. Sometimes loving someone meant talking about the failures just as much as the triumphs. True love could only be found in moments of honesty.

"I got it," Casper said, his voice sounding almost breathless with excitement.

"Huh?"

"The woman from the picture. Lois Trainer? She's from Columbia Falls. According to the FBI database, she's been in and around a series of major drug deals, but there's been no direct evidence linking her to the crimes."

"Do you think this is the woman we could be after? The woman from the shop?"

He exhaled, rubbing his hand over his face as he thought. "I don't know. I hope so, but knowing my luck, this lady probably doesn't know anything about it—and even if she did, she wouldn't tell us."

"You wanna try?" she asked, motioning toward the open road in front of them. "We can make a stop at her place. It's out of the way, but maybe we can dig up something."

Was it a coincidence that this woman lived just outside the park and was connected to the gang?

He looked over at Lex, his face was tight, making the fine lines around his eyes deepen. "It's gonna be about two hours, and after the accident... Are you sure you want to go?"

Was this his way to tell her that he didn't want her in the car, or was he worried that she was still mad? Maybe he wasn't as oblivious as she had assumed.

"What do you want? I mean, as far as you and I go, Casper?" she asked, putting him on the spot.

"I know you think I'm being evasive, that I don't want to open up to you, but that isn't the truth. The truth is that I've never been great at relationships."

"Why? What do you mean?" Finally, they were getting somewhere.

He reached over and sat his hand down softly between them, palm up, as if he wanted her to slip her fingers into his. But she wasn't ready to forgive him. Not yet.

"My last relationship ended just over a year ago. It was hard... Really hard..." He spoke gently, as if he were pulling memories from the deep, dark, off-limits part of his psyche. "I loved her."

"What happened?"

"Her name was Elicia. She worked with me in the FBI."

An ache grew in her gut as she jumped to a million different conclusions, each one worse than the last.

"She got pregnant when we were working together," Casper continued.

"With your baby?"

His eyes darkened and the scowl she hated returned to his face. "She said so, but later I found out that I wasn't the only man who she had been seeing."

She slowly let out her breath in an attempt to hide her surprise as pity filled her. No wonder he was so closed off, his emotions so out of reach.

"It was hard when I found out, but truth be told, in the world of the FBI, sex can be just as powerful a weapon as any gun. Sometimes to make things happen, a person has to sacrifice themselves for the greater good—at least that's what she told me."

"Did you believe her?"

He nodded, his movement so small it was almost imperceptible. "Her job was really hard. It meant going undercover and putting herself in places where she had to make tough calls—finding herself in places where she had to have sex with random dudes. I didn't blame her, but it definitely made things harder when…" He stopped.

"When what?" She reached over and placed her pinky inside his hand, letting him know that she was there, present, listening—and in a simple way, thanking him for his honesty.

"She lost the baby. She was on a mission in northern Washington. The guy she was after was a militia member. They were trying to talk him down and he went berserk—she took a hard hit. I'd told her that she shouldn't go out there, that she shouldn't put her life—and the baby's—on the line. She wouldn't listen."

"I'm so sorry, Casper." She instantly regretted asking him to share. From the pinched look on his face, it was easy to see why he was always finding ways to avoid his past.

"Don't be sorry, Lex. I killed him. I killed the man," he said, his voice barely above a whisper. "When I got to him, he didn't even have a gun. He was defenseless…just like my baby had been. And I gunned him down."

"How did you…"

"Stay out of jail?" he said, finishing her question. "The FBI kept my name out of the press and me out of trouble, saying it was in self-defense. But in truth I was pissed. I meant to kill him. He had bombed people, he killed my child—but in the end, I was no better than him."

"Is that why you're here?"

He nodded as his eyes welled with tears he fought to keep in check. "They told me I was a loose cannon—a liability. Truth is, I am. I can't stand by and just let the people I care about get hurt."

"You didn't *let* her get hurt. She made a choice and tragedy struck. You can't carry that weight. It wasn't your fault."

"I can, Lex. I will carry that forever. I'm a monster."

"You're not a monster, Casper. You took a bad man off the streets. It may have been against the law, or outside what the FBI wanted you to do, but sometimes there's a gray area between what is right and what is legal." She moved her hand into his, stroking his fingers like they were those of a child. "You did what you thought was right. From what you told me, I think you were justified."

"Justified or not, you need to stay away from me. I don't want anything to happen to you. You have to focus on yourself. You don't want me in your life. I only bring pain."

"Lucky for you, pain is something I'm used to," she said, thinking back to her days when she'd lived with her biological parents. She could still see the crack pipes, stained with brown, on the only table in their house.

No matter how strong he was, she saw him for what he really was—a broken man. With each other's support and honesty, just maybe they could grow beyond their pasts.

Chapter Nine

The mobile home was tucked into the back of a park, out of sight from the road and hidden by a flurry of overgrown trees. If it hadn't been for a small white arbor, complete with the drooping, tired heads of the last-of-summer flowers, Casper wouldn't have noticed the house they were looking for.

Getting out of the car, they made their way up to the small porch, the steps sagging with too much age and too little care.

"Why don't you wait back here? We don't know what we're going to find. This woman has a reputation that could make her dangerous." He stopped himself from saying, *and I don't want you to get hurt.*

No doubt by now Lex had to know that he was always protective of the people he cared about, and the more time they spent together, the more he cared about her.

Lex moved to speak but stopped and nodded, staying at the bottom of the steps. "Be careful."

Contented warmth spread through him, the kind that followed on the heels of realizing that someone cared and appreciated the way that he felt. Maybe there could be something more to what they had besides a simple friendship and passing work, but he hated to get his hopes up.

He knocked, the sound echoing through the thin, flimsy door. A dog started to bark from inside the place, followed by the sounds of a woman yelling for it to shut up. There was the metallic clang like that of a recliner being put down and then the steady thump of footfalls.

"Who in the hell is it? If you're selling something, I have a gun and I ain't afraid to use it," the woman yelled, her voice hoarse and raspy like that of a longtime smoker.

She threw open the door, letting it slam into the wall next to her. A small, mixed-breed dog that looked more like an overgrown ferret came running out and started to jump around Casper's feet.

He leaned down to pet the dog, and for a moment it was quiet as it sniffed him, and then it started its high-pitched bark again. The dog jumped on him, bumping his hand like it wanted to be pet, but it skittered away when he moved to touch it.

"Burt, leave 'im alone," the woman ordered, but the dog didn't listen. Instead it continued its dance between wanting love and wanting to defend.

The woman's hair was pulled up into a clip, wild with little brushing and infrequent washing, and as she stepped toward him he could make out the strong odor of cigarettes mixed with the stench of poor hygiene. He had envisioned the woman to be tough, but she looked tough for all the wrong reasons. The expression "ridden hard and put away wet" came to mind.

"Miss Trainer?"

"Who're you?"

"My name is Casper Lawrence. I was hoping I could ask you a few questions about a recent disappearance in Glacier National Park."

She frowned like she had no idea what he was talking about. "I don't know nothin'. Why're you here? How did you find me?" She stepped out onto the porch and closed the door behind her, blocking their view from whatever else lay inside. Her slew of questions made him wonder if she was the kind of woman who frequently had people looking for her.

"Like I said, we just want to ask you a few questions," he said. "Do you know of anyone who has gone missing in the last few weeks? A man?"

She looked toward the dog that had run down

the stairs to sniff at Lex. For a minute the animal was quiet. "I don't know about no man and nothing about the park."

He nodded. "What do you know about the local motorcycle clubs?"

Her body went stiff and her nostrils flared. "Look, if you don't got no warrant, and I ain't under arrest, I don't gotta answer nothin' about the Keepers."

"That's true, Ms. Trainer, but the last thing we want to do is come back and bother you again. We were just hoping you could be helpful and we could be back on our way. However, if you don't wish to help us, I'm sure that we could make a return visit—one that involves handcuffs. Don't you think we could avoid all that? I just have a few little questions. Nothing that's going to get you into any kind of trouble."

Ms. Trainer reached down and instinctively ran her hands over her wrists, like she was recounting the last time she'd been shackled. "I don't have anything to do with the Keepers."

The mere fact that the woman called the MC by its shortened moniker made it clear that she was lying. Very few people had heard of the club, and even fewer knew it by that name.

He took out his phone and pulled up the picture with her and Peter Kagger. "If that's true, Ms.

Trainer, then why are you in this picture with the secretary of the club—a man who currently sits in a Canadian prison for his implication in a series of crimes involving the MC?"

She paled. "That...that was a long time ago."

He tapped on the date. "According to this, this picture was only taken a few months ago." He looked toward Lex, who was scratching away behind the ears of the now-quiet dog. "Lex, do you think a few months is a long time?"

She glanced up at him. "Well, Casper, it depends on what we are talking about. A few months isn't long in terms of a lifetime, but it's a long time if it's hours spent in prison."

"You haven't been in prison lately, have you, Ms. Trainer?" he asked, not even attempting to mask the implicit threat that lay just under the surface of his words.

"Do I need to call my lawyer?"

He waved her off. "Of course not. Lawyers only make things more complicated for both of us. When you lawyer up it's hard to say how things will go, but I can guarantee that it wouldn't be as friendly as it is right now. It's my hope that you can make this easy—on both of us."

"Fine. I dated that guy. It wasn't a major thing. When he came to town, we got together," Ms. Trainer said, but from the way her eyes lit up as she spoke about the man, he could tell she wasn't telling him the truth.

"How often did he come to town?"

"Well, he's from Alberta. I guess I saw him a few times a month. When he could make it down."

"Why was he coming to the United States?"

She clapped her hands, calling the dog, but the dog ignored her.

"Ma'am?" he repeated, though he knew full well that she was just trying to think up some kind of convenient lie.

"He came down to see me. It's what people do in a relationship. Isn't that right, Lex? Ain't that what people do when they are dating?" she asked, motioning with her chin toward Casper.

Lex jumped slightly at the sound of the woman saying her name, or maybe it was the question, he couldn't be sure. "I'm afraid I don't know what you're talking about," Lex said, visibly taken aback at the woman's assumption that they were dating.

"You guys aren't an item?" She gave him an assessing glance. "You know, you can fake a lot of things, but you can't fake when you like someone. I see how you keep looking at her, Agent Lawrence."

He felt the warmth rush to his face, but tried to dispel it along with thoughts about how much he cared about Lex, and how she felt in his arms. He wasn't here to talk about his relationship or be interrogated by the woman they had come to question. She was the one under observation, not them.

"It's hard not being around someone you care about—which makes me wonder why you and Peter weren't together all the time." He attempted to steer the conversation back to the task at hand. "Based on this photograph I would guess that this man was someone who you cared deeply about. Why else would you have stood beside him on the court steps?"

Ms. Trainer studied her feet. "What does my relationship to Peter have to do with a missing person in the park?"

He smiled at her admission that there was more between her and the man than she'd wanted to say. "We believe that the man who went missing was a member of the same MC as Peter. We were hoping that perhaps you could help us shine a little more light on his identity."

"What do you want to know?"

Did that mean she knew the man whose remains currently resided at the Missoula Crime Lab?

"We took a picture of his bike. I was hoping you could tell me whether or not it belongs to him." He carefully sidestepped around the man's name, hoping that she would inadvertently take the bait and supply them with the information they needed.

He pulled up the picture of the bike as it was being loaded onto the flatbed.

She sucked in a breath. "Son of a—"

"Is this his bike?"

She looked up at him with eyes wide with shock, and at their centers he was sure he saw the fires of anger. But why would she be angry at seeing the picture?

"Sure, that's Razor's bike. Where'd you find it?"

Razor? Was that the name of the man whose body they found? He needed more than the strange nickname to go on.

"We found it at the trailhead where it was believed Razor started his hike into the park."

He carefully avoided telling her that the man he was asking about was likely dead—he didn't want to create a situation that would raise alarm within the biker community any more than he was likely to already be doing. If they knew the man was dead, none of them would help their cause, but if they thought the man was simply missing, they were far more likely to aid in the investigation.

"Do you know why he was hiking through the park?" Lex asked, stepping up onto the bottom stair. The dog was now in her arms and licking her face.

"Burt likes you," the woman said. "He don't like nobody but me—couldn't stand Peter. What did you do to him, feed him some uppers?"

Lex laughed, and the soft sound nearly made Casper forget what they were doing. He loved that laugh, that simple sound that made his heart reawaken.

"Wait—he did like Billy. One time he let him pick him up, but that was a couple of years ago," Ms. Trainer continued.

"Billy?" Lex asked with a confused look.

"Razor," the woman replied, but any softness she had shown when she looked at her dog was quickly replaced by an air of suspicion. "Who did you say you were?" she asked Lex.

"My name is Alexis Finch. I'm a park ranger and I'm working with Agent Lawrence on this investigation."

"I thought you were just looking into a missing person's case." The woman glared at him like she was trying to weigh and measure him for truth.

"Yes, ma'am," he said. "Missing person's case. We're hoping that this investigation will take a happy turn and we can return Billy to his family."

The woman's scowl deepened. "You say *his family?*"

"Why yes, ma'am." As he spoke he could feel the sand of her acceptance shifting under his feet.

"You need to leave," she said, charging down the steps and pulling the little dog out of Lex's arms. "Don't you be coming back. If you got something to ask, you can ask my lawyer." She stomped up the steps, went inside and slammed the door behind her.

He could hear the click of the lock as she slid it shut. The dog started barking again, but instead of wondering if the dog was defending her, he suddenly wondered if the dog was really begging for them to take him home.

"Do you think the dog was named after Burt Reynolds?" she asked with a laugh.

"He was just furry enough to be him. But definitely the '70s version, not the current one," he joked.

He helped Lex into the car and took one look back at the vegetation-covered property before he got in and started to drive. He picked up his phone and dialed the medical examiner. After being handed off by a secretary, the medical examiner, Les Traver, answered.

"How's it going?" Casper asked as he steered the car back toward the park's entrance. "Have you had a chance to go over that Glacier Park body case yet?"

There was a rustle of fabric as Les must have moved the phone. "Actually, I was just going over the report. Interesting stuff."

"Did you find anything usable?" he asked, taking her hand. Her fingers were cold.

"There was a small imperfection on the man's right zygomatic arch. There was evidence of calcification, so he must have had some sort of injury to his cheek prior to his time of death."

Casper squeezed Lex's fingers. Between the wound and what Lois Trainer had given them—now they would only have to track someone down who could give them the man's full name and a positive ID.

"Have you had any luck in identifying the man?" Casper asked.

"We've started to look into dental records, but so far nothing has matched. You?"

"I'm not sure, but we have a lead. We are thinking he went by an alias 'Razor,' first name Billy, possibly William. He was involved with a motorcycle club called Hells Keepers."

"Great." Casper could hear Les scratching something on paper. "We can use that."

"If I find out more, or have a positive ID on this guy, I'll let you know."

"'Preciate it," Les said. "By the way, did you get a chance to really look at the remains?"

"I was involved in the recovery, why?"

"Did you look at the skull, particularly the left orbital cavity, near the sphenoid bone?"

"His eye socket? What about it?"

"Yes, his eye socket, near what would have been

his nose." Les gave a light chuckle at Casper's unscientific terminology. "Inside of it was a small hole."

He thought back to the grizzly prints that had littered the ground in and around the area where they had found the parts of the body. He had seen hundreds, if not thousands, of deaths and murder scenes, but Casper cringed at the thought of what this man's last moments must have been like with a bear possibly breathing down his neck.

"Is the hole consistent with an animal attack?"

"Based on the margins, it's clear that this was definitely a penetrating trauma of some sort, likely perimortem. At first, based on the coroner's report and how he documented the scene, I believed it was consistent with the type of injury that you would find in a bear attack."

"But then?" Casper pushed.

"When we looked closer, there were no other abrasions or marks on the bone—like what you would see caused by the animal's incisors. I ordered a set of X-rays of the skull and foot, and we found something interesting." Les paused. "We found what looks to be a fragmented bullet. Small caliber, in my humble opinion, something similar in size to that of a .22."

"Are you telling me that this guy didn't die from

a bear attack?" He felt the air seep from his body as he thought about all the things that this could mean.

"Due to the amount of damage that was done to the brain by the round, I believe that it was the cause of death. However, I can't rule out that this man was attacked. It just may not have been the final blow."

A wave of chills charged down his spine. This man may have had a horrific death—the kind of death that they made movies about. Casper glanced toward Lex, who was staring at him with a horrified look on her face, as though she could hear exactly what was being said.

"Based on the fact that there was no exit wound, when this round penetrated the skull it didn't enter at a high velocity."

"Which means—"

"He didn't shoot himself. There had to have been someone else who pulled the trigger."

He stayed silent as the news sank in. "Our guy was murdered," he said, breathless at the thought.

"I'll continue looking over the remains and running tox screens," Les continued. "Maybe I can pull something else out of this, but I have to tell you, this is one of the more gruesome sets of remains I've seen in a while. This one time, we had a guy who'd died in his apartment, midsummer…"

The man droned on about the gory details of his former case, but all Casper could think about was the skull he'd held in his hands, the feel of the oil from the man's bones on his gloves. His stomach roiled, threatening to empty, and he forced the images from his mind. Sometimes the strong just had to muscle past the things that made the average man pale.

"Least this guy's death makes for one heck of a story," Les continued with a dismissive chuckle. "Would've hated to be in his shoes." Les laughed at his stupid joke. "Gunshot wound and a bear mauling… It's like the double whammy of deaths. Hell of a way to go. I guess the fates wanted this guy double-dead."

Chapter Ten

There hadn't been a single day that she had thought about playing hooky from work. Lex loved her job, and the fact that each day she could help people and the occasional animal. In her line of work, she never knew what was coming around the next corner, and that level of spontaneity always made her come back for more. It wasn't just the normal nine-to-five where she was stuck in some cubicle with a heinous boss coming down on her. In fact, today was the first time Dragger had really said something to her that was less than cordial.

Yet she was tempted to call in and tell him that she wouldn't make it in tomorrow.

She snorted at the thought. That would go over like a ton of bricks. By the end of the phone call she'd have no job, no place to live and no way to help Casper solve the case. She'd have nothing.

But there was a nagging feeling in her gut that

told her she couldn't quit—she couldn't just let him take her back home for the night and leave things as up in the air as they were. She wanted—no, she *needed* to get to the bottom of this.

Maybe she could push the issue with Dragger that it was vital for them to figure out a way to stop the flow of drugs through their park—especially if it led to murder. They didn't need that kind of publicity. No doubt Dragger would simply tell her that nature would stop the drug running long before they could. And maybe he was right. Maybe this drug running had just been a one-time thing. Maybe she and Casper were doing nothing more than chasing rabbits.

He had to see that if and when the media got their hands on it, their office's role in the investigation would inevitably come into question. They'd have a royal storm on their hands if they didn't treat the situation delicately—there'd only been two other murders in the park's history. This would draw headlines. She had to make Dragger understand that this investigation had to come first.

She reached for her purse on the car's floor.

"What're you doing?" Casper asked, carefully keeping one eye on the road as they drove back toward the main park entrance.

"I'm going to call my boss. Maybe I can convince him to let me keep working on our investigation."

A look of concern flickered over Casper's face. "You can't. No, Lex. I don't want you to screw up your life over this. I want you to be at my side, but don't risk your job over this case. You're kidding yourself if you think calling in again is going to help anything—it'll only piss him off and put you on his radar."

"I don't get how winterizing is more important than letting me solve a murder. I just don't understand his thinking."

He reached over, putting his hand on her leg and slowly stroking her thigh. "Lex, I don't know how this thing is going to play out. For all we know, we might hit a dead end on this and never find who was behind this guy's murder—if that happened, would it be worth compromising your career? And don't get me started on your safety. You know how I feel about that. We're dealing with a biker gang here. If you want an idea of what they're capable of, all you need to do is take a look at Razor's body."

She hit the button on her phone that lit up its screen. They still had service.

"You're right, Casper," she said, staring at her wallpaper of the jagged Citadel Peak. "These guys are dangerous, but I'm not afraid. I'm not the kind of woman who passes the buck when things get hard. If I was, I wouldn't be working at one of the most rugged national parks in the United States. Instead I would have a safe little desk job. I want my life to be an adventure. I want to help people. Most of all, I want to make sure that justice is more than just lip service in this world. This is my way to make a difference."

She set her hand on his, stroking the lines that ran over the backs of his hands.

Casper nodded with a tired, handsome grin, the kind that told her he'd known what she was going to say and wasn't surprised. "I love that about you, Lex. I do. But you need to know exactly what you might be walking into with this. I don't want you to have unrealistic expectations."

Her thoughts moved to Travis. He had always accused her of living with "unrealistic expectations," no more so than when she had tried to talk to him about their relationship and how she had wanted it to be. It wasn't that she had wanted the perfect marriage, but at the very least she had wanted a marriage based on honesty and enough mutual respect that they would talk and work together to make their relationship stronger. Instead he had pulled further and further away anytime she had asked him about anything beyond their four walls or the simple events of their work. In the end, her "unrealistic expectations" for a marriage that was something more than her waiting for him had cost her the man she had once loved. Yet she was glad she hadn't let it go on. She couldn't have suffered any more of the deafening silence and the complacency.

"Don't say that, Casper. I know what I want. I know what I'm doing. Trust me," she said, her voice flecked with old hurt.

His eyes widened slightly, as if her words had caught him off guard.

She lifted her phone and dialed Dragger. He answered on the first ring.

"Are you ready to go to the chalet in the morning?" he said, his voice gruff and unwavering.

She thought about avoiding giving him a piece of her mind, but after telling Casper how strong she was, how she believed in herself and in her boss's ability to accept this, she couldn't back down. "Mr. Dragger, so glad to catch you. I just wanted to give you an update on the situation."

"Unless it's to tell me that you're ready to hand off the investigation, I don't want to hear it."

"That's exactly why I'm calling, sir. I think it would be ill-advised to pass this to someone else at this juncture."

"It's nothing more than a bear attack. Let it go—Travis is supposed to be working up there tomorrow and he will take care of the last bit of cleanup as far as this case goes. It's time for you to move on. We don't have time or the budget to deal with this right now. You are aware that our tourism rate fell twelve percent this year? This is going to cut into our budget significantly if we're not careful."

Her mouth dropped at the sound of Travis's name. There was no way she would let him take this from her. He had already taken so much.

"Actually, sir, I was calling to let you know that we've just talked to the medical examiner who was handling the remains."

"What about them?"

"According to him, sir, we're no longer dealing with an accidental death. I'm afraid to tell you he believes that this case is a homicide."

There was a moment of loud silence between them.

"Sir, I was hoping that, as this case has grown and the media will no doubt be involved, I could continue my work on furthering the efforts of the investigation," she said, stumbling over her words as she tried to make it sound as respectful but necessary as possible.

Dragger made a sucking noise. "I appreciate your enthusiasm and candor in this, Alexis. I do. However, that doesn't change the fact that I'm giving this to Travis and his guys. I want you to meet up with him in the morning at the ranger station. You can give him your notes and findings. He will do an adequate job, I'm sure. After your accident, I would hate for you to put yourself in harm's way any more than necessary." The tone of his voice was dry and threatening, a sharp contrast to what might have been caring words.

"I'm fine," she said, rolling her neck as if Dragger could see just how fine she was through the phone. "I'm not feeling dizzy. It was only a minor concussion."

"With that type of injury, you shouldn't be putting any more stress on your body." Dragger sighed loudly into the phone. "Don't fight me on this. No matter how this investigation plays out, this guy is dead—so don't risk harming yourself."

"You're right, sir," she said, "but the fact remains he was smuggling drugs across the border into our park and then was murdered. Who's to say something like this isn't going to happen again? If it gets out that we aren't doing everything in our power to stop murders within our borders, our tourism next year may drop even lower."

"This investigation isn't yours to worry about anymore, Alexis. Travis will get a handle on this, and winter waits for no one. If you don't have your butt up at the Sperry Chalet in the morning, I will consider that your resignation." He hung up the phone.

"That bastard," she said, throwing the phone into her purse. "He's giving this case to Travis… Travis. Can you freaking believe it?" She slammed her hand against the dashboard, making pain radiate up from her hand and into her arm.

Right now, he must have had his lips planted squarely on Dragger's butt in order to get this case. No doubt Travis begged him for it. He'd always been the kind of guy who wants all the glory.

This time she couldn't let him have it. She had to stop this from getting into Travis's hands, but if she didn't follow Dragger's orders she'd be fired, and then that was exactly where the case would end up. There was only one thing they could do— they had to get on top of this. They had to figure out who was behind the murder before she was supposed to meet up with Travis.

"Travis is going to be working with me?" Casper pointed at his chest as though he was as taken aback as she was by the information.

"Sounds like it. Aren't you the lucky one?"

Casper clenched the wheel.

"I have an idea," she said, sweeping through her memories for anything that could help their case. "There's a biker bar just north of us here in Columbia Falls. It's called The Pig Snout."

"The last thing you need right now, with your recent concussion, is to go tie a few on." Casper cocked an eyebrow as he looked over to her.

She smirked. "That's not what I was after, smarty-pants. It's a place where I've seen bikers hang out. I've never been in there. It may be nothing, but there're always Harleys parked out front. Maybe someone there will know something."

She was grasping at straws. Even if the bikers that hung out there were affiliated with an MC, there was little to no chance that they would give them any more information than Lois Trainer had, but she had to do something. She couldn't let Casper down, and she couldn't let her ex move in and screw up not only her investigation, but also whatever was happening between her and Casper. Nothing good could come of their budding romance if Casper was forced to work the investigation with her ex-husband.

BEFORE LONG, THEY were parked outside the bar. Its sign was missing some of its lights and it read nothing more than "Pig not." Its defunct sign matched the building perfectly, listing to the left as though it had seen a few too many drunken men stumble from its doors and was simply following their lead. The gravel parking lot was littered with a variety of bikes. She didn't know much about motorcycles, but a few looked like the ones that she always saw on the shows about choppers, with their too-long handlebars and their intricate detail work. One bike even had skulls machined into the chrome of its wheels.

She thought back to the paint job on Razor's bike. Two skulls. Was it possible that these guys were part of the same motorcycle club? Had Razor been here, at this bar, in the days before he was killed? Could one of these men be responsible for his death?

Her mind raced with unanswered questions, her gut roiling with nerves. If these men were involved with Razor in any way, she'd be walking into a snake's den. The men who made up the one-percenter motorcycle clubs were the type who didn't just think, but knew, that they were above the law. One word came to mind as she thought about biker gangs: hubris.

"Are you sure that you want to do this?" Casper asked, motioning toward the listing bar. "We could look more into the bag we found. Maybe it can tell us something about the guy and where he came from. Heck, maybe we can find the woman from The Prince and the Pea. Maybe she bought the bag or something."

It was a cop-out. He knew they wouldn't find anything from that bag. It was nothing more than a run-of-the-mill, every-survivalist-owns-one kind of bag. There had to be millions of those things in circulation around the country. It would be safer to go down that path, but she didn't have time for safe—she only had time for answers.

If nothing else, at least he hadn't warned her about her safety again. Maybe he was learning that she was tougher than she looked.

She opened the door and stepped out of the car. "You coming?" She hitched her thumb toward the bar. "I bet there's somebody in there who just can't wait to buy you a drink. Especially with that badge hanging from your waist." She nodded in its direction. "Just a suggestion, but you may want to leave that in the car."

He looked down with surprise, as if he had forgotten he'd put it on that morning. "Good idea. I'm sure we'd get a real warm welcome with me wearing it." He dropped the badge onto the dashboard and got out of the car.

"We may get one anyways." She led the way to the bar, keeping a comfortable distance between them in case any of the bikers saw them. As they approached the bar, she reached down her shirt and lifted her breasts so her cleavage could be seen just above her shirt line.

"What're you doing?" Casper asked, not taking his eyes off her hands.

"I'm going to get us the information we need one way or another. If anyone asks, you're my brother." She stopped. "Actually, why don't you hold back for a while, let me get a read on this place before you come in. While you're waiting, why don't you call your friend at the US Marshal Service and see if you can get more information on this Razor guy? Maybe they could at least get us his full name." She motioned for him to retreat and then opened the door and strode in, not waiting for him to respond.

Men were lined up at the bar. Most had beers in front of them, but a few had tumblers filled with dark amber liquid. Each had on a leather vest, or "cut" as she remembered them being called on television. On the back of the man closest to the door was a large patch. It was made up of the same image that had been on Razor's bike—two skulls and a snake wrapping its body beneath. Above the image were the words "Hells Keepers."

She'd found the right place. Now she just needed to find the right man.

As she started to make her way deeper into the bar, the conversations around her hushed.

There was a gray-haired man with a nearly white beard sitting at the far end, and he waved her over.

She looked back over her shoulder, but Casper

hadn't come in. Maybe she had made a mistake in not having him with her. At least she would have been afforded some level of protection from the bikers. Then again, she couldn't be weak now.

She picked her way over to the older man, trying to saunter as she moved through pushed-out chairs and steel-toed riding boots.

A thin bead of sweat rolled down her back, making her feel even more afraid. If they noticed her acting nervous or *off* they wouldn't give her anything, and it would only put her further into danger.

"How's it going, pretty lady?" he asked, motioning for her to take the unoccupied stool next to him.

He had a patch that read "Madness and Mayhem," and above it was one that read "Hells Keepers." On the other side of the vest were two patches: "President" and "Montana Chapter." There were a series of diamonds and letters over the rest of the front of his vest, but she had no idea what they all meant.

"It's goin' real good," she said, trying to act as innocent and as acquiescent as possible. "How about yourself? Long day riding?" She slipped onto the stool and the man motioned to the bartender.

"You want a beer?"

Drinking was a terrible idea, but she couldn't fail now.

"Sure, I'll take a beer."

The man nodded toward the bartender, who grabbed a glass, filling it under the tap and then sliding it down the bar.

She grabbed it like she had caught beers a thousand times, instead of just having seen the movement in the movies. In a way, the action made her feel even more like an outsider.

"What's a pretty lady like you doing at a place like this tonight? Your man get mad at you?"

She took a long sip of the cheap and bitter beer and forced it down. "Nah, just saw you guys were here. Thought I'd stop by."

"We were here, huh?" He looked back at the man standing behind them like he was in on some inside joke. "I haven't seen you around here before. You looking for someone specific?"

"Actually, I met a guy a while back. He said his name was Razor. You know him?" She cringed inwardly as she thought of exactly how and why she had met the man.

The president looked down the bar to another of his comrades and motioned for him to come closer. The man answered in a second, stepping so close to her left that she could smell the oil on his vest and his day-old sweat. The patch on his chest read "Sergeant at Arms."

"This lady here says she's looking for Razor. You seen him?"

She tried to get a read on the president's wind-burned face, but she couldn't tell if he meant the question in earnest or if it was his attempt at getting the man's guard up about her. Either way it made her palms dampen with nerves, and she took another swig of her beer.

"I ain't seen Razor in a while. He's been up north so far as I've heard. Then again, I ain't his babysitter. You want me to look into him for you?"

The president looked to her. "The fine lady was looking for him. How did you say you met?"

"I didn't," she said, as the drink made her start to believe she had inner strength enough to go toe-to-toe with the bikers beside her.

The president started to laugh, the sound as raspy and hard as him. "I see why he liked you. He was always going after women who liked to throw their weight around." He leaned in close. "You know, he ain't around, and if you're interested in throwing your weight somewhere, my way's always available."

She glanced down at his wedding band. "Your wife know you talk like that?"

"What my old lady don't know won't hurt her." He laughed again.

A man who had been sitting at a table near them stood up and walked over. He leaned in and whispered in the president's ear as he pointed to something on his phone. Luckily, he spoke just loud enough so that she could make out his words.

"Our runners want to rendezvous tomorrow. Nine o'clock at the normal location. What do you want me to tell them?" the man asked.

The president turned away from her for a minute. "This about the Blue?"

The man nodded.

"Tell them we got their money, and this time they'd better not let us down."

The man walked back to his chair, texting as he moved.

She glanced over her shoulder, wishing Casper had been there to hear the men's exchange. They had to be talking about the Canadian Blue, which meant they must have been planning some kind of buy. These could be the men Casper was looking for, the men who had a role in smuggling the drugs over the border.

Then again, if these bikers were the smugglers, then why would they be buying and not selling?

She moved to stand up, but the president grabbed her by the arm and forced her to sit back down.

"Don't you be going nowhere. I'm sorry about that interruption, little lady. Sometimes business comes before pleasure, but both come in their own time." He gave her a nasty wink.

Pleasure from her wouldn't be coming his way, ever.

"I don't want to be interfering with any of your business," she said, motioning toward the man on his phone.

"Oh, don't worry about him. That was nothing. Already taken care of." He shrugged her off. "Now, about you and Razor... I know you ain't his old lady."

"Oh yeah, how's that?" she retorted, trying to sound cute enough to cover her genuine interest.

"Well, he's already got one of those. So do you belong to his chapter or are you general club property?"

She wasn't anyone's property, nor would she ever become something people could own.

"I ain't nobody's nothing. I've just been seeing Razor around. He told me to stop by this week. Said he'd be in town. If you ain't seen him, I should be goin'." She tried to pull her arm out of his vise-like grip, but instead he only held on harder.

"If Razor told you to come here and you listened, then you might just be the kind of girl this club is looking for." He stared at her with his cold, dark eyes. "We ain't desperate for women," he said, nodding toward the billiards area where a swarm of girls stood around with a few men as they played pool. Each of the women had Daisy Duke shorts and tank tops that rested so low a sharp breeze could have caused a nip-slip. A few of them wore the leather vests like the men of the club, but they simply said "Property of the Keepers," and a couple had specific men's names. She stared at them, looking for a woman who matched the description the shopkeeper had given her and Casper at The Prince and the Pea, but in the poor light of the bar, it could have been any one of the brunettes.

"We're good to our girls," the president continued. "If you're interested, I'm sure that we could bring you in. Make you club property."

"Why would I want to do that?" she asked, trying not to sound completely affronted even though she inwardly blanched at the thought of what he offered.

"Our girls want for nothing. You could travel the world on the back of anybody's bike you wanted. Money ain't ever an issue. Protection ain't a problem. If you're runnin' from something, or someone, we can be just the men you're looking for."

She was running from a lot of things, but most of them rested in her past—terrifying memories of her days in foster care, and nights spent hiding in the closet out of fear of being beaten once again. Right now the only place she wanted to go was out the door.

"What makes you think I'm running from something?" she asked, twisting the pint in her hands.

He chuckled. "If you are coming in here, looking for a man like Razor, you have to be either looking for trouble or wanting protection. If it ain't protection that you wanted, then that only leaves trouble—and that, that's something I can give you plenty of." He leaned back and appraised her from behind. "I can probably give you more than you can handle."

That was it. She couldn't take it anymore. "Look, Pres," she said, standing up even though his fingers dug into her arm, "I don't want any of what you're selling. When Razor finds out what you are trying to do, he's going to come down on you like a ton of bricks."

The man threw his head back with a wicked, drunken laugh. "Lucky for you, I ain't worried about Razor finding out nothin'—it's awful hard to get mad when you're as cold as he is."

She pulled her arm from his grip and ran out the door. There was the sound of scraping bar stools behind her. Casper was in the car on his phone, waiting for her.

"Start the car!" she yelled, making the motion of a key turning.

He looked at her and frowned but started the car. His mouth opened as his gaze moved past her. She turned around just in time to see the president walk out the door.

She hurried into the car.

The president stood on the steps of the bar and stared at her, and then at Casper and his badge on the dashboard. The man pointed to her and then drew his fingers across his neck like a blade slicing through thin flesh.

Chapter Eleven

"What in the hell did you just do?" Casper seethed as he tore out of the parking lot and onto the highway.

"I didn't *do* anything. That was the problem." Lex looked back over her shoulder in the direction of the bar.

There was a group of men standing outside, watching them as they retreated.

"I thought you were just going in there to see if you could find anything out about Razor. How did you manage to get an entire group of bikers to chase you out of the bar?"

She turned back around and clicked on her seat belt. "Look, they didn't chase me out. I ran out. Entirely different thing."

"Okay, why did you have to run out, then?" He checked the rearview mirror one more time to make sure that there weren't any bikers following them. A thought struck him. "You think one of those guys is the one who followed us last night—right before the accident?"

She shrugged. "I don't know, but they were talking about Canadian Blue. They were making some plan to have a buy...or whatever you call it."

"What do you mean?"

"I was sitting with the president, and another guy came up to him. They are having a rendezvous tomorrow where they are planning on buying the Canadian Blue. At least I think so…"

"Do you know where?" The car lurched around the corner, the tires sliding on the wet pavement.

"You don't need to drive like a bat out of hell. They're not following us."

"Just like they weren't last time?" He readjusted the mirror. "I can't let you get hurt again."

"I'm not some fragile thing that you have to treat with gloved hands. I've lived this long on my own. I don't need you to protect me," she said, suddenly angry that once again they were having this argument.

"Look, I know you're strong. Have you ever stopped to think that maybe I'm the one who's not?"

She stopped. The thought hadn't crossed her mind. "What do you mean, Casper?"

"I told you about the baby, my girlfriend, my

past. I can't go through losing someone else that I care about." He glanced back again. "I shouldn't have let you go in there alone."

She fumbled for words.

He *cared* about her. He'd said it aloud. This changed everything. They were moving out of the safety of their friends-ish zone...well, friends-that-kissed zone. The thought of a relationship terrified her, but as she looked at his gold-flecked eyes and the concern for her that was strewn across his face, a sense of calm filled her. He wasn't one of the men from her past. He wasn't the type who was going to try and keep her in the dark. It would be a struggle for him to open up to her, but he was trying. He'd told her things that she doubted he had talked about in a long time.

She didn't know how to make him stop worrying, but one thing came to mind. He had opened up. Now maybe it was her turn.

"You know, before...you weren't wrong about me avoiding talking about things that really matter."

He glanced over at her as though he was wondering where this new line of conversation came from.

"I...I never lost a baby. I can't even begin to imagine how hard that must have been for you." She nibbled at her lip as she second-guessed herself. Maybe she should wait until things were more real between them, but if she avoided the truth any longer, it would only be that much harder to talk about when things got more serious—she didn't want to hide anything from him. He needed to know who she really was.

"It was hard… It didn't even matter whose baby it was. In my heart, it was mine. When she called me…" His grip tightened on the wheel. "There's no going back to the way things were before. You can't change the past."

"I know." She sighed. "I've tried."

"What do you mean?"

"When I was six years old, my birth parents were arrested. They'd been strung out for days. Neither of them had jobs. Most days I didn't eat and at night…nights were the worst." Memories of her mother and father screaming at one another filtered into her mind. "One night my mother tried to shoot my father. I ran to my neighbors and told them what happened."

Casper's mouth twitched with rage as he pulled his face into a tight scowl.

"I was taken by CPS and put into foster care. For seven years, I bounced around from one house to the next. Finally I landed on the Finches' doorstep and they were gracious enough to bring me in. For the first time in my life I had enough food, clothes and love. They changed my life."

He reached over and took her fingers in his and lifted their entwined hands to his mouth. Ever so gently, he kissed each of her fingers.

"For a long time, I fought back against their love. I didn't feel like I deserved it and I couldn't trust it. I couldn't accept that they wanted to just bring me joy and security—I'd learned early on that everything in life comes at a price."

"Do you still think that?" he asked, his hot breath caressing her fingers.

"I hate to say it, but I do." She twisted her mouth as she waited for him to chastise her for being so pessimistic.

Instead of disagreeing with her, he nodded. "Life makes us hard. Doesn't it?"

The truth was that she didn't want to be that way. She would give anything to be the kind of woman who could see the joy in other people just like she could see the true beauty of nature.

"Some prices are higher than others," she said. "And with some choices you have to continue paying for them for the rest of your life—even when the choice wasn't yours." As she said the words, it felt almost as if she was saying goodbye—as if no matter what happened between them, the vast plains of their pasts would be too immense for them to come together.

As they drove up to Lex's cabin, Ranger Grant was standing beside his truck, waiting for them. She was surprised to see the man, especially so late at night. Yet there he stood, leaning against the grille, arms folded over his khaki shirt that was pulled taut over his paunch belly. His hair was slicked down with too much gel in order to try and cover his balding top, but the attempt only made him look older.

In a way, she was relieved to see Grant—it meant that Casper couldn't just leave, he would have to stay and talk and he would be hers for at least a few more minutes.

She tried not to get her hopes up as she thought about her feelings of goodbye.

Grant walked up to the driver-side door and extended his hand to Casper as he got out. "Agent Lawrence?"

Casper looked confused and she realized that it was likely because he'd never actually met the man before. She rushed around to their side. "Casper, this is Ranger Grant. You spoke with him on the phone."

"It's great to meet you, Grant. Did you get a chance to look into the missing pills?"

Grant pushed his pudgy finger under the second

button of his stretched shirt. "Actually, that's why I came here. I was hoping to catch you."

"How did you know I was going to be here?" Casper asked, an air of suspicion in his voice.

"Oh, I just took a guess." Grant gave him a knowing smile. "But about the pills. I got in touch with a detective friend of mine in Kalispell. It sounds like they have started to make their way around the county."

"How does he know that these are the same pills and not from another shipment?" Casper asked.

"Truth be told, we don't," Grant said with a shrug. "But from what the detective said, they had been going through a little bit of a dry spell. Not much was on their radar, but then within twenty-four hours of your heist, the pills started showing up on the streets. It has to be more than a coincidence."

"Could they have been coming in from anywhere else?" she asked.

Grant shook his head. "This isn't like meth. It can't be found everywhere. This is a localized epidemic, with a local—or somewhat local—source. The farthest these pills reach, on average, is Eastern Washington, in and around Spokane, and they had moved east into North Dakota, mostly in the dying roughneck towns."

"So you think that this smuggling operation is

how the drugs are entering the country?" Casper asked, making Lex think back to the conversation they'd had with Steel.

"Without a doubt. If you drew a circle around where the drugs have been found, this would be the epicenter."

He'd been right.

Casper pulled down the brim of his hat, setting it tight on his head as he stood quietly. He looked at her with a questioning glance.

She nibbled nervously at her bottom lip. Until tonight, when they were in the middle of an investigation that was starting to pull them deeper and deeper into the shadows of society, Grant had never given her a reason not to trust him. But there was something about him, the fact that he knew where they were and when they'd be home, that made her nervous.

Chapter Twelve

Even though it was late summer, when they walked into her cabin the place was cold, and Lex was forced to start a fire. Normally this late in the season the weather was warm enough to keep the cabin heated, but a storm had settled into the mountain valley and had started to release its rain. Once again the place had started to take on the edge of cold that marked the onset of fall.

Time would slip by and she'd lose herself to the needs of the park. She looked out the window and watched as Casper stacked wood on his arm to help with the fire.

She sucked in a breath as he bent over to grab another log from the stack.

Casper stood up and, noticing her watching, gave her his provocative grin, the one that seemed to be only for her. His hat dripped as the light smatter of rain hit the surface and rolled off in small streams.

She'd never dated a man who wore a cowboy hat before, but watching him made her realize how sexy they were. They were the mark of a real man—a far cry from the bun-wearing men she often saw hiking through the park, or scattered across her social media feed.

Wait, were they dating?

No. She chastised herself. This was, in all probability, the last time they'd really spend together. She'd be handing her investigation off to Travis tomorrow and from there she and Casper would have no professional contact. She lived an hour and a half away from his post near Waterton—long-distance relationships never worked. Sure, they could see each other once or twice a week, maybe more in the beginning, but real life would take over, they would spend less and less time together, and soon there would be nothing between them but heartache and faded memories.

If they got together it would be doomed to fail from the very beginning.

She held open the door for him as he carried in the wood. He was breathing hard under the struggle of carrying all that weight.

"Thanks," she said, suddenly more aware than ever of the unwelcome feelings of desire that bubbled up within her. "It's nice to have an extra set of hands."

"No problem." He carefully set each piece of wood in the box a few feet from the potbelly stove.

He walked over to the fire and stoked the embers, even though they were fully alight with flames. "It should heat up in here in no time," he said, closing the stove and turning back to her. "But if you don't mind, I'm going to warm up before I go."

She couldn't help the smile that overtook her face at his lame excuse for wanting to be around her for a little longer. Was it possible that he was feeling the same confusing mess of emotions that she was?

"What about the bikers? What if they come here?" She nibbled seductively at her lip.

"I think you're okay. They didn't get your real name, did they?" he asked, almost as if he was oblivious to the fact that she was, in a way, asking him to spend the night.

He definitely wasn't a player, or there would have been no way he would have missed her pitch.

"I don't think so," she continued. "But I'd feel better if you stayed for a while. You know, just to make sure they don't come after me...or us."

Maybe his miss was a hit after all.

"About the bikers, why didn't you tell Grant

about the rendezvous tomorrow?" He moved slightly so he could face his palms toward the heat.

Lex walked over and stood beside him at the fire. She shrugged. "I dunno. It just didn't feel right, you know?"

"Are you worried that if you tell him, word will get to Travis?"

She hadn't thought of that, but Casper might have a point. If she had given Grant the information, it would make Travis's work significantly easier. She wasn't vindictive or glory-seeking, but it ate at her that he was taking over, and no doubt would get all the accolades when he solved the case.

"I'm going to have to tell Travis about what we found anyway, I guess."

"If that's not it, then what do you mean by, 'it didn't feel right'? Grant didn't seem like a bad guy. If anything, he was pretty helpful going out and talking to the local cops for us, and he combed the wreck—twice."

A thought struck her. "You're right. He did comb the scene of the wreck." She rushed to the tiny table by the kitchen and grabbed a piece of paper. She jabbed her pen into the soft paper as she wrote down a series of names.

"Look," she said, lifting the note for him to see. "These are all the people who knew we were carrying the drugs that night. Travis, Hal, the other ranger—John—and you and I. We were the only people on the scene of Razor's death."

"We talked about this. I don't see how those guys could be behind us losing the drugs."

"Think about it... Who all have Travis and John been talking to?"

Casper shook his head, not following her.

"I'm sure they've been talking to Grant." She ran her hands through her hair with excitement. "When they were taking off in the helicopter from the crime scene, Travis was on the phone. He was probably telling Grant about what we had found and where we were going with the drugs. Maybe they set up the accident. Then maybe Grant just picked up the pills."

"Are you serious? You think that Travis and Grant have something to do with our drugs getting stolen? It seems a little far-fetched."

She paused, staring at the yellow legal pad and its list of names. He might be right, but then again, there was a little part of her that couldn't accept it. "How did Grant know we were here tonight? That you were with me? The last people who saw us together were the bikers."

"So now you think the bikers are in Grant's pocket?" Casper took off his hat and threw it on her couch, just atop the quilt her foster mother had made her. "This isn't some episode of *Law and Order*. Everyone isn't in cahoots. There has to be a more simple explanation to all this."

"Why are you being so dismissive of my idea?" she asked, trying to keep her annoyance from seeping into her voice.

"I'm not being dismissive. I just don't think the entire ranger district is involved with a biker gang. I mean, take yourself, for example. You were married to Travis. Did either of you have bikers stopping by? Was there anything at all before this started to make you think he, or anyone you know, has been working with the MC?"

She sighed, setting the pad back down on the table. "Maybe you're right. I'm getting ahead of myself. It's just…I want to get to the bottom of this."

"Everything's going to be okay, even if we don't solve this tonight." Casper walked over and stopped behind her. He started to rub her shoulders. It felt so good, the kneading pressure of his fingers in her taut muscles. She hadn't realized how stressed she was. "You know, at least something good came from all this."

She opened her eyes and looked back at him. "What's that?"

"I got the chance to meet you. You're the best

thing that's happened to me in years." He leaned down and his lips met hers in one glorious kiss.

Her body flushed to life. It felt so right as his tongue brushed against her lower lip and she tasted the mint on his breath. She turned around, not breaking their kiss. Reaching up, she ran her fingers through his slightly-too-long locks.

His hair was so soft, it felt like strands of silk in her fingers. She pulled him harder against her lips. She wanted more. So much more.

Even so, there was a warning that sounded from the back of her mind. For a moment she paid it heed, but quickly doused the negative sparks with the euphoric wave of his kiss. She could have this. Him. Here. Now.

Consequences and the future be damned.

She was an adult woman. A woman with needs. A woman with wants. And right now the thing she wanted most was pressing against her, his body responding in a way that proved he wanted her as badly as she wanted him.

He pulled her into his arms. His shirt was wet and he smelled of pine and sweat all laced with the heady aroma of lustful pheromones. If she was forced to think of the sexiest scent on the planet, it would have been him, in this moment.

She trailed her fingertips down from his hair and over the rough stubble that riddled his cheeks.

Drawing back, she ran her thumb over the slightly chapped skin of his lower lip. Playfully, he took her finger into his mouth and traced his tongue just over the tip. He nibbled it and she drew back at the surprising mix of pain and craving.

Lifting his hand from her waist, she mimicked his movement, sucking and pulling his finger into her mouth. Deep and long. Licking the length and stroking it with her lips. On his fingertip was a bump and he winced slightly as she swirled her tongue on the spot. She stopped.

"Are you okay?" she asked, looking at the place on his finger that she had felt with her mouth.

There was a small dot and the skin around it was raised and angry.

"Don't worry about it," he said, slightly breathless.

She smiled as she thought of how she had made him feel.

"What happened here?" she asked, attempting to prolong the agony of desire.

"I poked my finger when I was sewing your pants. It's no biggie. Really," he said, leaning in to take her mouth again, but she pulled back.

"You mended my pants?"

"Yeah, your work ones. The ones you ripped on the log."

"When?"

He sighed and stood tall, as though he realized that she was playing hard to get. "I mended them when you were asleep in the hospital."

She stepped out of his arms, going to the laundry basket in the bathroom and taking out the pants. There was a small series of stitches, perfectly aligned and set. It was better than she could have done. In fact, if she hadn't known better, she would have thought a professional had done the work.

He walked into the room behind her and leaned against the door frame. "Up to snuff?" He gave her that roguish grin she loved so much and she dropped the pants back into the basket.

"Even better." She took him by the hand and led him to her bed.

It melted her heart as she thought of him sitting beside her, setting to work on her pants. There was something so hot about this alpha-type man sewing. Thinking of her broken man taking care of her in such a selfless and domestic way made any last shred of doubt about him slip away.

He checked every box that she wanted in a man—strong, smart, sweet, caring, not afraid to speak his mind and not afraid to admit when he was wrong. He was the unicorn that every woman wanted. And he was hers.

She reached up and started unbuttoning his shirt.

"What're you doing?" he asked.

"You took care of me, now I take care of you." She gave him an impish grin. "We need to get these wet clothes off. I don't want you catching your death of cold."

He laughed. "I see…" He sucked in a breath as her hands moved to the lowest buttons of his shirt and she skimmed the rough fabric of the front of his pants.

She loved this game and relished the thought of making him long for her.

Slipping his shirt from his shoulders, he stood there, his body reflecting the orange flickering light of the fire. He had a thin patch of hair between his pecs, just enough for her to run her fingers through without being too much.

Stepping closer, she took his nipple into her mouth and sucked, making a popping sound as she moved to the next. His breathing intensified, and his hot breath slipped down her neck and under her shirt like a caressing touch, making her nipples as hard as those in her mouth.

He pulled her up to him, taking control. He fumbled with the buttons on her shirt, but in his state, his fingers seemed to be disconnected from his body. He gave up and ripped it off, sending buttons flying throughout the room.

"It's a good thing you know how to sew," she joked.

His smirk returned, but this time his eyes were burning with red-hot desire that made her core clench and the dampness grow between her thighs.

He unbuttoned her pants and let them fall onto the growing heap of clothes. Gently he lifted her onto the bed, laying her head on the pillow. "Are you okay?" he asked, as if touching her hair had suddenly reminded him of their accident.

Some of the heat disappeared in his eyes and she longed for it to come back.

"Don't worry about me. Right now let's just be here, in this moment." She unbuttoned his pants.

His body arched around her touch as if he was shy, but wanted more. Ever so slowly, she lowered her hand, tracing her fingers down his length. The fire in his eyes raged once again.

She pushed his pants and boxers off.

He moved between her legs and lowered himself into her. Her body pulsed with life and she moaned at the beautiful torture of feeling him inside her.

If she had her way, this night would last forever.

Chapter Thirteen

As Lex arrived at the ranger station the next morning, her body ached with the pleasant pain that came after a long night of lovemaking. She smiled as she thought of their time together, him between her thighs, and the feeling of her head on his chest. Her mind swam in the warm thoughts of what the future could bring, until her friend Kelly stepped out from the back office and stopped at the front desk.

Her work friend was in her midthirties, petite but a bit on the heavy side, and on the cuff of her shirt there was peanut butter smeared where one of her kids had used her as a napkin.

"Lex, what're you doing here?" she asked. "I thought you were still recovering. I was going to stop by and see you after I got off work today."

"Dragger wanted me back—wants me to button up Sperry."

"Are you serious? Dragger called you back? He couldn't have meant it after what happened. Did they ever figure out who forced you off the road?"

Lex shook her head and, not for the first time that day, she wished Casper was still with her. She had made him stay behind and look further into the bikers.

"No one's come forward and we can't track down any witnesses. Grant's helping us." She paused. "By chance, have you talked to him lately?"

Kelly nodded. "He called me last night and asked me where you were. Apparently he was looking for you—did you guys catch up?"

So, Casper had been right. Grant had been telling the truth and had just luckily tracked them down. She felt silly for suspecting that everyone around her was guilty. Maybe she was just losing her mind; or maybe her past was conflicting with her present.

It was a wonder that Casper wanted anything to do with her and her baggage. Maybe he just didn't know what he was getting himself into. Or maybe last night had been his attempt at a one-time thing. A sliver of panic moved through her. Had last night been just that—a one-night stand?

"Are you okay?" Kelly asked, almost as if she could read her mind.

She plastered a fake smile on her face and nodded, but Kelly kept looking at her as though she didn't believe her.

Travis's voice echoed out from the back office, but she couldn't tell whom he was talking to.

She couldn't even fake a smile as she heard him.

He was laughing at some unheard joke as he stepped out into the main office. He gave her a smug grin as he spotted her. "I thought you were going to quit."

So he'd been talking to Dragger at some point? She shouldn't have been surprised. Why had Dragger told Travis about his threat to fire her? Travis had no business knowing anything about her or her options.

"Oh, I'm sorry to disappoint," she said, trying to summon every bit of self-confidence that she could muster.

Dragger and John walked out from the back office. John, the blond ranger from the recovery, was strutting like a fat goose as he looked at her.

"What's wrong with you?" she asked as John stuffed his thumbs into his pockets.

"John here," Dragger said, motioning toward the man, "will be taking over the case."

"But—but you said it was going to be Travis who took over," she stammered as she stared in disbelief at her ex-husband.

"I changed my mind," Dragger said with a dismissive shrug. "He asked to go with you up to Sperry instead."

"What in the hell? Why did you do that, Travis?" Who did he think he was to push his way back into her life?

"Whether we are married or not, Lex, I care about you—not like that CBP agent you've been running with the last few days. There's no way that after your accident I'm just going to let you go up to the chalet and spend the whole day working all by yourself. It's a recipe for disaster."

Travis had never been the kind for grand gestures, and when they'd been together he'd never gone out of his way to make sure that she was okay. If anything, most things had revolved around him and his needs—especially when it came to "his time." There had to be something else going on, something that he wasn't telling her.

"First, Travis, you don't *let* me do anything. If I go up there, it's my choice to make and not yours. Second, why the sudden change of heart? You don't give two shakes about me."

Dragger stuffed his toe into the thin industrial carpet as he tried to look at anything but her.

Travis rolled his eyes, and the stupid adolescent response made her want to pitch her shoe at him. She had every right to get upset. He didn't love her. He hadn't loved her in a long time. Just like his showing up at the hospital, it was nothing more than a show.

"Lex, I've always loved you." He reached over and tried to touch her, but she batted his hand away in disgust.

"If you loved me, Travis, then why did you treat me like you did?"

Kelly smiled from behind the desk and gave her a little thumbs-up, as if she was enjoying the show that was happening in front of her.

"Knock it off, you two," Dragger ordered. "You have plenty of time to hash out your private business on the ride up to Sperry."

She considered being petulant and telling Dragger that she refused to work with Travis, but from the sour look on Dragger's face, it would only end in her being reprimanded—or worse.

"I want you to take the pack horses and use Gunsight Trail. Check that all the hikers are out so we can close the trail," Dragger ordered, looking to Travis and giving a quick nod of the head like they had some private agreement. "Before you go, Alexis, you need to fill John in on all your findings with the case. Where's Agent Lawrence? I thought he was going to be here to pick up his new partner."

She was happier than ever that she had told Casper to cut and run.

"I have no idea where he's at, sir," she said, not entirely lying. All that mattered now was that he was making the most of what little time he had before John interfered.

CASPER CLOSED HIS eyes and leaned his head against the car's window as he let last night's memories flash through his mind. Their bodies entangled in a mess of arms and legs, wet with sweat and smelling of sex. His body shuttered to life, but he tried to ignore it. He was one lucky son of a gun.

He had imagined that a night with her would be hot, but she had been even better than his best fantasies. It had been one hell of a way to spend the night—and if he had his way, it was exactly where he'd like to spend the entirety of his life. If he did, he would die a happy man.

There was a knock on his window and he opened his eyes to see Deputy Steel standing outside the car, staring at him.

"Are we gonna work or just hang out and nap all day?" Steel asked, his voice muffled by the glass.

"Get in," Casper ordered, half laughing as he motioned to the passenger seat. "I've been waiting for you nearly all day. I thought you must have gotten lost. I know that's a problem for the Marshal Service."

"Sorry, your mom made me breakfast after last night," Steel ribbed.

Casper laughed. "It's just like old times. You're just lucky I'm feeling nice."

Steel thumped down into the seat next to him. "You're never this nice… Apparently you've been on your own too long in that little shack on the border." Steel leaned back and took out a notepad. "So, you told me about the bikers. Anything else I need to know?"

"Lex has been worrying about the people around her. I don't know if there's anything to the way she's feeling, or if she's being overly suspicious, but I think it's worth looking into."

"Lex?"

"Alexis Finch, the ranger I've been working with on the investigation, but her boss took her off today. I'm supposed to be getting a new partner from them. That's why I'm out here waiting for your sorry butt."

"Why did she get taken off the case? Were you guys sleeping together?"

He couldn't help the heat that rushed into his face.

Steel glanced over at him and his mouth opened with surprise. "You were? You dirty dog."

"It isn't like that. I swear. There's no way they

could have known. It just happened. They took her off the assignment before things ever heated up between us."

Steel raised an eyebrow. "So that's why you are feeling so nice?"

"This doesn't go any further than you and me. I don't kiss and tell."

"Good policy," Steel said. "My lips are zipped."

Casper gave him an appreciative nod.

"So your girlfriend—"

"She's not my girlfriend," Casper interrupted.

"Okay, so your not-a-girlfriend friend, Lex, is suspicious about her coworkers. Did you tell her that you thought there might be something to her feelings?"

"I'm not sure that there is something there. I mean, there's some other things involved that may be affecting her judgment."

"Like what?"

"Like she works with her ex-husband."

"They get along enough that they can work together?" Steel asked.

"Not really."

Steel nodded as if he finally understood why Casper felt the way he did.

"She just texted me. Sounds like she is going to have to spend the day with him deep in the park."

"Oh," Steel said. "I bet she's happy about it."

Steel leaned forward and pulled a laptop out of his bag. The thing was one of those huge computers that was equipped with industrial-strength plastic and a bulletproof shell. Secretly, Casper kind of wished that he had one like it. "I had my guys follow your friends, the Keepers, last night in an attempt to find out who, and where, they were going to meet today. I had to call in more than my fair share of favors on that one."

"Appreciate it, man. This will all come together, and you'll see that all your hard work was worth it."

Steel motioned for him to start driving. "Head toward Columbia Falls."

Casper pushed the car into gear. "What's up there?"

"It sounds like they had another shipment of the Canadian Blue come through."

"From where?"

Steel got a cheese-eating grin on his face. "The bikers are meeting up with someone at the back entrance to Glacier—the unmanned gate. We weren't able to make out who they were meeting, but—like you assumed—it's our belief that whoever is selling them the drugs is bringing the pills over the border and through the park."

"Do you want me to call in some backup so we're not on our own at this buy?"

"You don't like the ten-bikers-to-one-Fed kind of odds? Come on now, if there are any more of us it's almost unfair to them…"

Steel laughed, but the pit in Casper's stomach deepened. He'd never been afraid of facing bikers or any number of adversaries, but they had threatened Lex, and after what had happened last night with her…well, for once it felt like he had something—or someone—to live for.

"Don't you think it would be—"

"Hey now, Lawrence," Steel said, interrupting him. "I was just kidding. Three other marshals are going to meet us up there. We got a line on the president of the club. Three years ago he escaped the federal pen. According to our man, he's going to be at the buy. Hopefully you and I both get something that will help our careers."

Casper twitched. It wasn't a surprise that Steel knew he'd had trouble in the past, but he hadn't thought the guy would bring it up.

"That's why you're going after this like your ass is on fire, isn't it? So you can get your foot back in the door with the FBI?" Steel pressed.

Honestly, he hadn't thought of it in those terms, but Steel wasn't wrong. If he played his cards right—if he could take down an international drug-smuggling ring—it would look good on his résumé if he decided to go after his former job.

He sucked in a long breath as he thought about it. He wouldn't have to live in the middle of nowhere. His days wouldn't be an endless flow of checking bags and passports and the infrequent investigation. He wouldn't be the low man on the totem pole.

But if he went back to the FBI, he would likely be transferred out of Montana—and away from Lex.

There's no way they could make it work—the distance would be too far, and his life would fall back into the constant flux that came with a job in the FBI. His days would be filled with investigations and reports, and his nights would be filled with thoughts of what he could do better. He'd fallen into this trap before. He couldn't do it again—he couldn't give up his life, his chance at happiness, just to get a foot up at the Bureau.

As he drove, he thought back to the feel of Lex in his arms. Everything about last night seemed like a dream, every action a snippet held up in the surreal fog of too-good-to-be-real; her hair tickling his chest as she sat atop him, the feel of her hips in his hands, her feet entwined with his.

All this season, he had thought of the standalone station at Goat Haunt as his place of imprisonment, but maybe it wasn't a prison after all—maybe it was a chance for a new beginning.

It was all so confusing. He had thought he'd hated this place, but in the last few days everything had changed.

If he told Lex about the opportunity the case could provide, would she want him to use it to his every advantage, or would she urge him to stay near her?

He imagined the look on her face if he told her that he wanted to go back to the FBI. It made something in his chest shift. He couldn't live with himself if he broke her heart. Hell, just the thought of leaving her broke his.

He shook the thoughts from his head. He was playing in the world of what-ifs anyway. Before he'd ever have to make any decisions, they would have to get a handle on the investigation. They needed to find direct evidence that tied these bikers to the drug trade, and they needed to find out exactly why and how they were running the drugs through the park—and they needed to find out who murdered Razor.

"Grant met up with me last night," Casper said. "He let me know that there was Canadian Blue hitting the streets in and around Kalispell. He thinks they're the drugs that were stolen from my truck."

"No crap?" Steel said. "He have any clue who stole them?"

Casper shook his head. "He's no closer to finding out, but my gut is telling me that the answer's right at our fingertips."

"What do you mean?"

"The night of our accident, there was a biker following us." He tapped his fingers against the steering wheel as he attempted to pick his words very carefully. "I know it's circumstantial, but everything about this case revolves around that MC and the men in it. I'd bet my bottom dollar that they set the whole thing up. Maybe they knew we had the drugs. Maybe they knew we were taking them back to Apgar to the evidence unit. So they picked a spot on that road and forced us off it."

"You think that they wanted to kill you guys?"

A wave of nausea passed over him as he contemplated the thought, but he swallowed it back. "If they wanted us dead, they would've killed us… They could have done it right then and there."

"Is there a reason they didn't?"

He thought back to that night. When they'd hit the rock wall, he'd lost consciousness. When he'd come to, they had been surrounded by bystanders. "There were a lot of witnesses."

"It sounds like you guys are lucky." Steel whistled through his teeth. "If these guys are as bad as I think they are, and they're behind the murder and the drug running, it would have been a win for them to take you and Alexis out. You were two of only a few people that could point a finger in their direction."

Chapter Fourteen

The chestnut mare's hooves clicked against the rocks as they climbed higher and higher up Gunsight Trail and closer to Sperry Chalet. The timber was intermittent as their elevation grew and, on the leeward side of the mountain, the horses had to fight through a thin layer of snow and ice on the trail.

Her horse pulled in a deep breath, making Lex's legs widen around her girth, and giving a long huff as if growing as tired of the hike as Lex was. Travis had been quiet most of the way, but as they drew nearer to their destination he had started to talk more and more.

"Do you remember that one time when we found the woman? You know, the one who died in the creek?" Travis asked as they passed by a small waterfall cascading out of a small crevice in the rocky hillside.

She tried to hold back the image that came to the front of her mind of the woman's blue lips and her clouded, sightless eyes. For a long time she had seen that face every time she had closed her eyes and tried to go to sleep.

"Travis, do we really have to talk about her?" she said, turning in her saddle slightly so she could look back at him over her shoulder.

He shrugged. "Just thought we could make conversation."

"Is that why you got me pulled off the case, so we could *make conversation*? Did it ever occur to you that I was *this close* to solving it?" She pinched her fingers together to emphasize her point.

"Trust me, you weren't that close, and besides, I'm not the one who got you pulled off the case."

"Then who did?"

Travis smirked. "You and your big mouth did that all on your own."

"What do you mean by that?" Rage steamed up within her.

"Nothing… I don't mean anything." Travis sighed. "Look, I didn't come with you to start a fight."

There was a strange inflection in his words as if he were holding back…or hiding something.

"This isn't your attempt to get back together,

is it?" she asked, trying to finally address the elephant in the room.

Travis laughed, the noise echoing through the steep ravine and cascading down to the valley below—making it sound almost sinister.

"You and I were never meant to be, Lex. I know that now. You're too good."

"Too good? I've heard some stupid excuses before, Travis, but *too good*? That's a new one."

They came over top of a small rise and the cabin, made out of a collection of multicolored natural stones, came into view. It was encompassed by a stand of timber, making it look like something out of a Tolkien book instead of a real place.

"Remember the last time we were up here?" Travis asked.

Her horse nickered and its ears swiveled as if it was trying to catch a sound to its left. The horse didn't like something. She was becoming nervous, stumbling slightly as she grew more wary.

Lex reached down and patted the horse's neck. "It's okay, baby," she cooed, trying to calm the animal. "It's okay."

She looked around, trying to see what exactly had spooked the horse, but she couldn't see anything that would cause the animal to react like this.

She glanced behind them at Travis's black-and-white gelding sidestepping on the narrow trail as he tried to get him to keep moving forward.

"Stop, Travis. Don't push him. He's scared," she said, forcing her voice to be as calm and neutral as possible in an effort to keep the horses from getting more spooked.

Travis stopped moving the reins and sat still in the saddle.

Her mare stiffened beneath her, lifting her nose and drawing in a breath, trying to catch a scent in the air. She blew it out with a huff and nickered again, the sound high with fear.

"Was anyone supposed to be up here?"

Travis shook his head. "Everyone was supposed to be out. The last paying guest checked out yesterday."

She nudged the mare, trying to get her to move forward, but the animal refused to budge and instead started to scoot her feet backward toward the edge of the narrow trail.

"Whoa, baby… Whoa." She pulled up on the reins and the horse stopped inches from disaster.

Lex lifted her foot out of the stirrup, sliding her body out of the saddle and dropping to the ground, the motion slow and even. "It's okay, baby," she cooed, her full attention on the scared horse.

She moved around to the front of the mare, out of its way in case it decided to spook. "Come on, baby, move away from the edge," she said, gently tugging on the reins in an effort to get the horse to step forward and follow her.

They weren't far from the cabin. If she could just get the animal closer to the safety and protection of the structure, maybe it would calm down.

The mare moved after her a few steps and then its eyes grew wide with fear. She reared up and squealed, pulling back on the reins and tearing them from Lex's hands. Turning, she charged down the trail, disappearing from view.

Travis was fighting with his gelding, trying to get it from following after the loose mare. As he pulled on the horse's reins, it skittered sideways. It jumped, its back humping like a bucking bronco, throwing Travis to the ground in a heap. His foot caught in the stirrup and the gelding turned and started after the mare, dragging Travis a few feet, his leg in an inconceivable angle, before he broke free.

She held her breath as Travis lay motionless on the ground. His foot was at an obtuse angle from his leg, broken. There was a thin trail of blood where his body had been dragged over the angular, jutting scree that littered the trail.

"Travis," she said, her voice frantic. "Are you okay?"

She moved toward him, stopping as she came

close. She didn't want to touch him too much. If he'd broken his back or his neck she couldn't risk moving him.

"Travis?"

He remained silent and unmoving.

What if he was dead?

She kneeled down and pressed her fingers to his neck. There was the slow, steady *thump, thump, thump* of his heartbeat, but he was seriously hurt. He needed help. Now.

She pulled out her phone. No service.

Maybe Travis's phone would have some bars. Ever so carefully, she reached around and flipped back the bottom flap of his jacket so she could reach in the coat's pocket. Her fingers brushed against cold steel.

There, just beneath his armpit in its holster, was a small silver revolver.

They had come up here to close down the cabin. Why was he carrying a gun? In all the time they'd been married, she'd never known him to carry a gun, except when he was on a call or when he was going to put an animal down.

Aside from their horses, she was the only animal here.

She pulled the gun from his holster and slid it into the back of her waistband.

Maybe she had this all wrong. Casper had told

her that she was overreacting in being suspicious about everyone…maybe he was right. There had to be a legitimate reason for Travis to be carrying the gun.

Right now she just had to get him the help that he so desperately needed.

She reached back into his pocket, grabbing his phone. A plastic bag dropped on the ground as she took out the cell.

Inside the bag was a collection of blue pills—at least twenty, maybe thirty of them.

She gasped.

What in the hell was going on?

Someone grabbed her from behind and pulled the gun from her waistband. Their hand moved over her mouth, stifling her scream.

"Shut your mouth, Alexis," a man whispered in her ear, raising the barrel of the gun until the cold metal brushed against her temple. "If you want to live, you will shut your face and listen."

"PETER KAGGER, THE secretary for the Keepers' Alberta chapter, is willing to help us, but he wants extradition to the United States and to have his conviction expunged from his record once he arrives." Steel motioned toward the phone in his hands.

"What else does he want? A freaking gold star

award? This guy shot a Canadian senator. We have zero jurisdiction there, and little leverage. How in the heck does he think we're going to be able to honor his requests?"

"He has two years left on his sentence and he says he's an American citizen."

"Oh, that's even better. How did an American shooting a Canadian senator not hit every news-reel from here to London? If he thinks that we are going to cause a possible international uproar by sticking our necks out for him just because he may or may not have information that will help our murder case, then he's got another thing coming."

Steel chuckled. "I hear you, but he's the only open door we got when it comes to finding any-thing out about the biker gang." He pointed to-ward the line of bikes that were parked outside Moose's Pizza Joint in Kalispell. "I don't see us barging in there and walking out with the infor-mation we need unless we make some sort of deal. I got friends in the Canadian Parliament. Maybe they can pull some strings."

Just on the other side of the windows, two bik-ers were standing guard at each side of the door. Since they had arrived the bikers hadn't stopped watching them.

They had to find out who was behind this mess and exactly what role the bikers had in all of it.

"Tell him we need some information to take to a federal judge. If he gives us something we can use, maybe we can see what we can do to bring him back to the old red, white and blue."

Steel went back to his phone. Inside the pizza joint, an older man with a black cut stood up and looked out the window, directly at Casper. The man had a goatee smattered with silver and black that made him look like a snarling dog as he spoke. The sinister look made every hair on Casper's arms rise, but he refused to look away. Just like a wild animal, the moment you turned your back was the moment they would attack.

Casper lifted his hand in an amicable two-finger wave.

"What in the hell are you doing?" Steel growled as he hung up the phone.

"Did you get us anything?"

Steel reached over and pulled Casper's arm down and out of view. "According to Kagger, that man you're making buddy-buddy with is the Montana chapter's president. He wouldn't give me a whole lot of details about the guy, but I'm sure that he isn't the kind you are going to be knitting sweaters with."

"Did Kagger know anything about Razor's murder?"

The chapter president walked over to the men

by the door, and they kept glancing over their shoulders toward Casper's car.

"According to Kagger, their MC wasn't behind the hit. He said the gang wouldn't have touched him. From the word on the street, Razor was basically a made guy. He was the president's right-hand man—did all his dirty business. If anyone touched him, there would have been a holy war."

"Then why is the gang sitting around having pizza if that's true?"

"Razor was in the Alberta chapter, not the Montana one, but Kagger said these guys are on the hunt for the killer, as well. He said that none of the clubs have a positive ID on the shooter—and they're willing to do just about anything in order to get a name. This could be our way in."

Steel slipped his cell phone into the breast pocket of his white button-up. "And if they get their hands on the shooter before we do, you better believe that it's likely we'll never know about it—or, if we do, it will be only because we'll be on clean-up duty."

The glass door opened and one of the guys who had been standing guard slowly sauntered out toward them. He had on the same leather cut as the other men in the restaurant, but instead of the normal rockers he only had one that read "Pledge."

So the president had sent an expendable. Casper

had a nagging feeling that things were about to get ugly.

"You wanna call for backup?" Casper asked, nodding toward the man who was making his way across the parking lot toward them.

"I think we can handle ourselves here. The last thing these guys want is a bloodbath in their back-yard. These are one-percenters—they believe in the live-and-let-live ideal when it comes to law enforcement—especially Feds." Steel forced a smile as the man drew nearer.

Casper couldn't ignore the tension in his friend's voice and the way his hand instinctively moved to the holster under his left arm.

The man walked over to Casper's window and waited for him to lower it completely. He must have had a WWE wrestler as a father and an Amazonian as a mother. His neck bulged with muscles, and the leather cut he wore creaked under the strain of his wide chest as he breathed.

"Howdy, son," Casper said, greeting him as though the man was a lap dog instead of a pit bull.

"Son?" The man looked behind him and then turned back with a dangerous grin. "I ain't your son."

A thousand smart-assed rebuttals sprang to the front of his mind, but he bit his tongue. "No offense. How can we help you?"

The man readjusted his cut. "My friend in there—" he jabbed his thumb in the direction of the pizza joint "—he's wondering why you are following us."

"We're not following you."

"Bull," the man said, his voice taking on a steely edge that only promised problems. "Ever since your little girlfriend came in our club last night, we've had a tail—until you arrived it was the US Marshals. We ain't stupid."

Casper glanced over to Steel, who gave him an acknowledging tilt of the head.

"Is that why you guys called off your rendezvous with your buyers today?" Casper pressed.

The guy's eyebrow rose like a large, hairy caterpillar. "I got no idea what you all are talkin' about. We don't got nothing to do with no drugs. We just were hungry for the best pizza in town." He smiled, the action making his sunburned skin pull so tight across his chapped lips with the unaccustomed motion that they cracked. Little specks of blood dotted his lips. "In fact, you guys been out here a long time…watching us. I bet you're hungry. Why don't you both step inside?"

From the tone of the man's voice, it was clear that it wasn't a request.

"We're all good here," Steel said, either not

picking up on the man's order, or else he'd chosen to ignore it.

The man put his hand up. "Just going for my phone," he said as he reached into his pocket.

Casper's hand tightened on the grip of his gun. "Make sure to move real slow, or your vest will be air-conditioned."

Steel tapped his fingers on his holstered sidearm, and the man nodded.

"I ain't here to threaten you. Ain't in none of our best interests." He slowly pulled out his cell phone and opened up something on the screen. "Especially when we all just want what's best for your little friend."

He lifted the phone so they could see, and on the middle of the screen was Lex. Her hands were tied behind her back and her eyes were covered with a blindfold. A trail of blood dripped down the side of her face.

"What did you do?"

"I didn't do nothing. Someone's trying to make things right by killing your woman in our name." The man's smile disappeared, and he licked the blood from his lips. "I think it's best if you come on inside."

He turned around and started to walk toward the restaurant. Steel and Casper hurried to follow.

"Where was she supposed to be?"

"Her boss had her riding into a high-mountain cabin today. She left at six this morning."

"Would she have been there by now?" Steel asked.

She'd told him they were taking the Gunsight Trail, but that meant the trek would have been over thirteen miles. It would have been a long ride, maybe six hours. He glanced down at his watch.

"She could've made it to the chalet by now, sure. But how do we know that's where she's at?"

"Did you see her this morning?"

Casper nodded.

"And you are sure that she made it to work? These guys couldn't have gotten their hands on her?"

"I didn't escort her to the ranger station, but she texted me. She sounded fine. Nothing out of the norm."

"You mean other than the fact she was pulled off a murder investigation, just when things were heating up?"

Casper slammed the car door shut. "You make it sound like this is somehow my fault. Like I shouldn't have let her go to work this morning."

Steel shook his head. "You should know as well as I do that sometimes the best tool we've got in an investigation is our intuition. She told you that she felt she couldn't trust people, yet you just let her go. Now here we are. For all we know, she's a thousand miles from here… Hell, she could be in Canada right now. You should have stayed at her side."

"You don't know her at all if you think she was going to let me stand guard all day. Don't you think it killed me that I left her this morning? If I could go back and do this all over, I would. I love her, damn it. I thought I was protecting her by making her go back to work."

"If you love her, then you better make this right. You may be the only one who can save her life."

Chapter Fifteen

The president of the MC sat at the table in the corner of the restaurant, his fingers tented in front of him as if he grew impatient, waiting for them to sit down.

"Did my guy tell you what we have on the table here?" the president asked, his voice was hoarse with age and hard living.

"If you touch a damned hair on her head, I swear I will come down on you like you've never seen. Not only will you spend the rest of your life getting the full treatment in the federal pen, I'll make sure that no one in your entire club will ever sit on a motorcycle again. The only thing their butts will touch will be whatever gets to them at the various federal lockups across the country."

"Whoa now, man," the president said, putting his hands up in surrender. "You got me all wrong. We didn't do nothing to your little girlfriend.

Though, I gotta admit she's a fine piece of work. You're a lucky man if you're tapping her."

"Don't talk about her like that," Casper seethed. "Where in the hell is she? I want to know now, or every federal officer in the state of Montana will be here in a matter of minutes."

"Hey now, Agent Lawrence, don't make threats that your job can't deliver. We both know that you being a CBP brings about as much authority as a mall security guard."

"Shut up," Steel interrupted. "You're a damned idiot if you think that this is how you are going to go about getting us to see your side of things. If you're not careful, Agent Lawrence is right. You and your comrades here will be seeing the inside of your jail cells by nightfall. So keep talking crap if you got nowhere else to be, otherwise tell us where we can find Lex and who's got her."

The president threw back his head with a loud laugh. "Whoa, I thought we were out of the loop on this one. You do know the man up there, the body you all found, is one of ours, right? That's why you stopped by our place and played your Hail Mary last night, correct?"

Steel glanced over at him. It had been a long shot, coming into their bar, but they had been desperate to move the case forward. Now, looking back, Casper wished they'd done anything besides draw the gang's scrutiny. He'd screwed up and gotten Lex in trouble—all over a dead gang member and some drugs.

They were never going to stop the flow of drugs into the country, at least, not on their own. They had been naive to think they could handle this case—that they could actually make a difference.

He'd thought things were going to be different when he'd left the FBI, but here he was back at square one, the people he cared about getting hurt and being put in danger, just for some illusion that they could make a lick of difference.

A waitress walked up to their table, oblivious to the turmoil that was roiling through him. "Can I get you all something to drink?"

Casper shook his head, so upset that he could barely think, let alone speak.

"They'll both have Cokes. Put it on my tab, darling," the president said, giving her a quick smack on the butt as she turned and walked away. "And hurry up with my pizza…you don't want us to start eating you up."

The girl giggled at the terrible come-on and the sound made Casper's stomach sour. "Where is she? Where's Lex?"

"Sit down."

The president's guards pulled out the chairs for him and Steel and they both sat.

The president waited to speak again until after the waitress had disappeared back into the kitchen. "I want to make it clear—we didn't have nothing to do with your old lady's disappearance. If anything, we tried to talk them down. But they only see her as a bargaining chip. She got too close to the fire. There's only one way out for her."

"What are you talking about?" Casper asked, his mouth dry.

"She pissed off the wrong people. There's little we can do."

"Who did she piss off?" Steel pressed.

"If I talk, Kagger walks free, and we get full impunity. You don't get to come after us for what's happening to your old lady. We ain't responsible."

"Why would we agree to that?" Steel leaned back in the chair, using his body language to take the power position in their negotiations.

"Come on now, we all know that you are at my mercy. If you guys don't act fast, not only will every shred of your case disappear, but they're going to kill your woman. You guys don't want more blood on your hands, do you? Don't you think you've had enough in the past?"

"My past isn't up for discussion. Just tell us where Lex is," Casper ordered, his voice full of panic as he moved to stand up.

The guard behind him pushed him back into his

seat. "You ain't goin' nowhere. Not until he says so," the guard said, looking at the man in charge.

The president nodded, turning to Steel. "Do you know what kind of man you work with? Your man here lost his job at the FBI over a woman. Apparently he lost it when the woman he'd fallen in love with had an affair, got pregnant and then lost the baby—he killed the guy responsible in cold blood."

Steel nodded. "I'm aware. It's a low blow to think you can manipulate a federal agent. Besides, take a close look at how you live your life. Are you really in a position where you should be throwing stones?"

"I just want to make sure that you are aware that your buddy here thinks with his heart and not with his head—at least not the right head."

Casper jumped up, moving out of the guard's hands. "Where is she?" He reached down and grabbed his gun and pointed it at the president, taking aim right between the bastard's eyes. "Tell me where she's at, right now, or you're a dead man. You know I'm not bluffing." The gun was unwavering in his hand.

Steel moved behind him, pulling out his gun and flagging the men, moving them back and protecting Casper's six.

"If you shoot, Lawrence, you and Steel are going to be as dead as me in a matter of seconds.

Then who's going to save Alexis? Use your head," the president said, not batting an eye.

"Tell us where she is, and we'll agree to your deal. You guys have impunity."

"You'll drop your drug charges against us and anything else you are brewing up?" the president asked.

"Drug charges? So you admit that you've been running the Canadian Blue over the border?"

The president snorted with derision.

"These guys are the ones who stole the Blue from my truck. They knew I didn't have enough proof or pull to come after them." Casper was numb. "Which one of you stole the drugs?"

The president tilted his head toward a guy standing to his right. The man looked hard, like the rest of his comrades, and wore a bandanna around his head.

"Don't forget, boys—full impunity here. You break your word…and, well, you don't want to know what we'll do to you and your friends."

"Who was the woman who helped Razor in Waterton? Was that Lois Trainer?"

"Lois? She told me you stopped by her place. Gave her a little scare."

"Was she the one with Razor?"

The president shook his head, but some of the

color drained from his face. "You don't need to worry about that girl who was with Razor. She's young and innocent."

"But Lois isn't?"

The president didn't answer.

"Lois is your distributor, isn't she?" Casper shook his head as he thought back to the woman's trailer and the little dog. No wonder they had scared her. He and Lex had been at her house the day after the drugs had been stolen, and the pills were probably just inside Lois's door—it's why she hadn't wanted them to see inside, why she had been in the picture with Kagger and why they were all so desperate to have the guy out of jail.

If Casper's gut was right, Kagger wasn't just another member of the club, but only time would tell.

"Using these women is how these guys have managed to stay off the radar for so long," Casper continued. "They use their women to handle anything that might attract too much public attention. If everything had gone right, no one would have known anything about Razor or his involvement. Instead he got himself shot."

"Ding. Ding. Ding. We have a winner," the president said. "At least one of you knows his ass from a teakettle. You will not come after us—or Lois—with any charges. You got it?"

"Fine, you got impunity from any pending charges, that's it," Casper said. "But know this, if we catch you running drugs over the border again, we'll rain down on you with the full fury of the federal government. Do you understand?"

"Us, running the drugs over the border?" He laughed. "You really are in over your heads. No wonder Lex is up there at that chalet…you guys have no idea. You got no clue who your real enemies are."

THE FEAR HELICOPTER cut through the air, slicing around the ridges and valleys that surrounded Lake McDonald. It was a short flight to the chalet, but between getting the helicopter and working things out with the MC, Casper already felt like they had taken too long. Lex's life was in danger and no one in the world could move fast enough to comfort him.

"Tapping your foot isn't going to make the pilot move this piece of metal any quicker," Steel shouted into his mouthpiece, the sound echoing through the speakers in Casper's helmet.

"If we don't get there soon, I'm going to stick my feet out and Flintstone this mother," he said, but the joke was as rigid with fear and angst as the rest of him.

Steel laughed.

Every time Casper closed his eyes, the only thing he could see was Lex, her hands tied behind her back, the blindfold and that thin line of blood. Whoever had thought they could hurt her and get away with it had another thing coming.

"You thinking about the bikers?" Steel asked, pulling him out of the nightmare of his thoughts. "We're lucky they wanted to talk to us. It's amazing what happens when you're the highest bidder."

"Sure," Casper said, looking out the window as they flew over the crystal-clear lake. "I know I should feel lucky, thankful even…but it just doesn't sit right. We weren't that close to bringing down charges on them for stealing the Blue, or for selling drugs. It just wasn't enough motivation to drive them to work with us. There has to be something else going on here."

Steel gave him a knowing look. "Let's not look this gift horse in the mouth."

He was right, but that didn't make the knot in Casper's gut disappear. "This's going to come back and bite us in the ass—you don't need to lose your job over this."

"And neither do you."

"My job doesn't matter. The only thing that I care about right now is getting Lex back safe and unharmed. If she's hurt… You might have to put the cuffs on me yourself."

Steel drew in a long breath. "Whatever happens up there, Lawrence, we're in this together. Thick and thin, I got your back."

Chapter Sixteen

The world was black, and for a surreal moment Lex wondered if this was what it was like to be in the world of the blind. She drew in a breath, pulling the scent of pine and earth deep into her lungs. Wherever she was, it didn't carry the mineral-rich aroma of heated rock, or the leftover greasy scents of cooking that always seemed to permeate the chalet at the end of the season.

A damp chill wafted against her skin. Was she outside? No. She sat back slightly and her back brushed up against crumbling dirt. Sliding her foot to the right, it hit a wall. She had to be enclosed, but where?

Maybe in a place with an opening…somewhere that let in natural air. Perhaps a cave?

She racked her brain, trying to think of a cave that she knew of near the chalet, but nothing came to mind.

Her hands ached from being tied behind her back, and she tugged at the rough rope, but it only made slivers of the rope dig farther into her skin. Her wrists burned, but she kept moving, and the rope loosened incrementally.

"Sit still," a man ordered. She thought she recognized the voice, but she couldn't put a name to it.

A wave of light slipped through her blindfold as the man's footsteps shuffled on the dirt floor. He must have been standing in a doorway.

The pump house. They were keeping her in the chalet's pump house, but why? Were they hiding her? Was there someone coming, or was the place simply the first thing they had thought of to keep her out of sight?

She tucked her feet under her.

"I told you to sit still. If I have to tell you again, you'll get another lump on your head."

She stopped moving. Her fingers brushed against the edge of her pant leg. Running her fingers up the leg, she touched the L-shaped hole that Casper had mended. She pinched it between her thumb and forefinger and rolled it back and forth. In a strange way, the simple action calmed her and her thoughts wandered to Casper.

He couldn't possibly know what was going on here. She barely knew what was happening—or why. There wasn't a single chance that anyone was going to come save her. Whatever happened was up to her. She had to be strong. She traced the stitches. Casper was with her, at least in spirit. She could feel him there, just as if he was beside her.

"Why am I here?" she asked the man who was standing guard.

"Shut up. You're not here to talk. You're just making this harder on yourself."

She couldn't understand that in any way. He was the one making it hard on her. He was the one who had kidnapped her. None of this was her fault.

Waiting a few minutes, she spoke up again. "How's Travis?" The question was simple and decidedly safe—or so she hoped.

The man shuffled his feet as though he was trying to decide whether or not to answer her.

"Is he alive?" she pressed.

"Travis'll be fine, and a heck of a lot better off than you."

"Did you get him medical attention? It looked like he broke his ankle. He needs to see someone as soon as possible."

"Look, Lex, if you were smart, the person you'd be worried about here is yourself. Yours is the ass that's really on the line."

"Who are you?" she asked.

He snickered. "If you stopped to think about anyone besides yourself and the little melodrama you've had over the last few years with Travis, you'd know exactly who I am…and maybe why you're here. As it is, you and your stupid attitude have gotten you nothing but trouble. Now it's time you paid."

"My attitude?"

Normally, when it came to her job, she kept to herself. It kept her out of the politics and away from the gossip mill. If anything, her attitude had been a healthy thing—especially when she and Travis had gone through their divorce.

"You always thought you were so much better than everyone. They all call you Wonder Woman behind your back, you know that, right?"

"What?"

"Yeah, if there's some amazing feat that needs to be done, we just call Wonder Woman. You always make a point of having all the answers. You're so self-righteous. You never screw anything up. It's freaking annoying."

She wasn't following his logic in the slightest. "If I'm so-called Wonder Woman, then why did Dragger pull me off the case?" As she spoke, a thought struck her. Had Dragger pulled her because he *didn't* want her to solve it? Was he somehow involved in all of this?

The man laughed again, the sound low and menacing. "You can ask him yourself when he comes back. From what I hear, it may be the last chance you'll get to talk to anyone, so you better make sure you ask any questions you want answers to 'cause the only person you'll be talkin' to is God himself when Dragger's done."

She couldn't think of anything that she'd ever done to make Dragger hate her. Why would he want to kill her?

"You guys don't have to kill me. I don't know anything. I won't talk to anyone." She hated begging, but panic filled her. "I promise."

"You are too much of a Goody Two-shoes to make me actually buy in to what you're saying. You couldn't even let the bear-mauling go." The man must have leaned against the door frame— she heard wood creaking beneath him. "Just think about it. If you'd just let things go and let our guys do what they do, the case would have been done and over with. You could be safe now. But no. You always have to go the extra mile. You always have to make the rest of us look bad."

"You look bad all on your own, John," she said, finally placing the man's voice.

"Screw you, Alexis." The man didn't deny his identity. He was the other ranger who'd helped re-cover Razor's body.

This must have had to do with her investigation, but how? What did he and Dragger have to do with it?

She rolled Casper's mend between her fingers. Silently, she wished he was here. He'd know how to get them out of this mess.

Outside, there was the sound of Travis's voice. He sounded upset, his tone deep and dark, but she couldn't quite make out his words.

"Is Travis okay?" she asked, hoping this time John would give her more.

"Your ex-husband is just fine. He just needs to shut his damned mouth." John moved, the light shining through her blindfold again.

"Don't kill her. We already paid the MC—they got what they wanted. There has to be another way to get around this. There has to be," Travis shouted.

"What's he talking about?" Lex asked. She moved to her left, and her body rubbed against the cold rock wall.

"Don't worry about it," John growled. "Don't move. I'll be right back." He stepped out and there was the sound of a door slamming behind him.

She was back in the blinding darkness. Her only company was her nagging fear that the next time the door opened, death would be there to greet her.

THEY LOWERED THE HELICOPTER, the stone-sided chalet growing larger as they neared. A man stood out in the only flat area and raised a rifle. He shouted something, but they couldn't hear him above the sound of the chopping blades and the motor.

The pilot glanced down. "You guys know him?"

"No," Casper said, his voice grainy in the mic.

"Either he's going to have to move, or we're not going to be able to land. I did see another small clearing we could use, but it's about a mile back."

"No. We're not leaving her here with these men any longer than necessary. Land this sucker."

The pilot gave him a stiff nod, but even behind his sun visor, Casper could see the strain in his face.

The man beneath them motioned for someone else, and another man, a taller one, with wider shoulders and a paunch belly sauntered out of the chalet. He took one look at them and flipped them the bird.

"Huh, so we're not going to get the royal welcome," Steel said, pulling out his sidearm and motioning for Casper to do the same. "If you want to save her, we may have to fight."

"With two of them out there in our landing zone, there's no way I'm going to be able to get any lower—and if they start shooting, I'm going to have to bug out. We can't put the bird at risk. Not if we want to make it out of this alive," the pilot said.

At their feet was a long rope, the type used for rappelling.

"You up for the ride of a lifetime?" Casper asked Steel, motioning toward the rope.

"I haven't done that since my training at Glynco. I guess it's about time to brush up on my skills," Steel said with a laugh.

They hurried to put on their rigging and Casper took his position at the door. "You got my six?"

Steel nodded. "You better hit the ground with a round in the chamber. Right now they are like trapped animals. It's going to be hard to tell what they'll do. They're desperate."

Steel hadn't needed to tell him. He was more than aware how deep they were in this. One mistake and none of them would make it to the end of the day. They would disappear, or become "victims of a helicopter accident," and no one besides the men responsible would be the wiser.

Casper jumped out the door. The rope whirred through his hands until he was far enough from the copter to slow his descent, but even then the rope burned his skin. He needed to get down there, get his boots on the ground and save the woman he loved.

A bullet zinged through the air and the copter pitched to the left, dragging Casper off course and forcing him to hang on to the rope for the lifeline it was. Steel was sitting at the copter's door, his legs out, taking aim at the men who'd tried to wing him.

His shot cracked through the air.

Casper slipped down the rope, taking the momentary cover that Steel was providing.

His feet touched the ground and he unclipped from the rope and pulled out his gun. There, just out of range, stood the man who'd been on the mountainside when they'd recovered Razor's body. John. The bastard pointed his gun at him, but the man next to him grabbed him by the arm and shook his head, motioning toward the helicopter and Steel. "Take them out first," the man yelled.

"You got it, Dragger!" The man took aim and his shot split through the air. There was a metallic tang as it struck the bird.

Dragger… Alexis's boss? He was in on this?

White-hot rage burned through him.

It made perfect sense. It was why he'd sent Lex up on the longest and most dangerous trail to the chalet, and it was why he called her off the case… Ultimately, everything came back to him.

Casper had been so stupid in letting Lex walk into the trap her coworkers had created.

Sometimes your worst enemies were those you thought were your friends.

Dragger took aim at the helicopter, but before he could squeeze off a shot, the helicopter cut to the left and whipped out of the hot zone. They moved west, likely toward the safe landing area a mile away. Casper was on his own. Alone with two gunmen.

Two men with guns were never going to be enough to stop him, not when it came to saving Lex.

"Lower your weapons!" He raised his gun over the top of the rock, taking aim squarely at Dragger's center of mass. "I can guarantee that this isn't going to end well for you if you don't put down your guns."

John looked over at Dragger like he was waiting for an order, but Dragger didn't budge.

"Look, Lawrence, you don't have to get wrapped up in all of this. This doesn't concern you."

"It does concern me. You don't get to kidnap the woman I care about and then expect that I'm not going to gut you."

"Gut us?" Dragger laughed. "In case you didn't notice, you're outmanned and outgunned. You don't have a snowball's chance in hell of making it out of this alive. So why don't you play it smart and listen to what I have to offer… Or we can just

kill you now and get it over with. Your choice."
He flagged the gun in Casper's general direction
as he spoke.

Casper was within his rights to pull the trigger
and kill Dragger, but he held back—this wasn't
like the last time he pulled the trigger. He only saw
two men, but that didn't mean that there weren't
more men in the wings…or with Lex. If he took
the shot, it wasn't just his life at risk—he might be
putting Lex even further into danger.

"What do you want from me?" Casper asked.

"See, I told you he'd come around, boss," John
said.

Dragger shut him up with the wave of a hand.
"Why did you come up here, Lawrence?"

He thought for a moment before he answered,
fully aware that the wrong answer could end up
getting him killed. "I wanted to save Lex."

"It wasn't to cart us off to prison?"

It was, without a single doubt, but he held back
from saying so. "My main concern is Lex. I need
to know she's safe before we can discuss anything
else. Got it?"

Dragger turned to John. "Go get her."

John ran off in the direction of a small building
east of the chalet.

"You didn't really answer my question, Lawrence. Don't think I didn't notice." Dragger low-

ered his gun slightly, almost as if his arm was growing tired. "How did you know we were here?"

"The tooth fairy told me."

"Told you what, exactly?" Dragger gave him an appraising look as if he were trying to understand how much trouble he was in.

There was untapped potential in his ignorance. For once, it wasn't Casper who was in the dark— and he could play this to his advantage and maybe get the confession he needed to bring this guy and his crew to justice.

"I heard all about your dealings, Dragger. You have one heck of a racket going. How much money did you pull in this summer running the Canadian Blue?"

"We would have gotten a whole lot more if you hadn't gotten in the way."

"How much did we cost you?" Casper continued.

"Close to 140k."

"That's just a drop in the bucket over the summer, isn't it?"

"Our Canadian friends charged us for the loss of their guy and they took our cut. They're threatening to take their business elsewhere. In order to make things right, we told them we'd take care of the loose ends—starting with Lex. Once she's gone, killing you should be easy."

"Assuming I'll let you hurt her is one hell of a mistake."

"Whether you believe me or not, I don't want to see her killed. She's a good ranger, but if we don't do something to make things right with our business partners, in the end it's the park that suffers. Half of that money goes into our budget."

Casper didn't believe him—Dragger was no Robin Hood antihero no matter how badly he wanted to convince himself he was. He was a criminal, and more than likely every cent they made landed squarely in his pocket. "Let's cut the bull. I know you're not giving the park the money. You're lining your own pockets."

Dragger smirked. "If you're capable of keeping your mouth shut, you could, too. You could make our whole process a hell of a lot easier. It'd be nice to have someone at the border helping us bring our supplies across. We could quadruple our business."

"Depends on what's on the table."

Dragger glanced over at the little building near the chalet. The front door opened and John dragged Lex out by her bound wrists. Casper rushed in their direction, putting himself directly in the line of fire—but he didn't care.

"Take your damned hands off her." He pushed John out of the way and ripped off Lex's blindfold. He fumbled with the knot of rope at her wrists, but finally managed to break her free. Her wrists were red and raw. "You had no right to treat her like this."

John stepped back, a look of fear crossing his face.

"Lex, are you okay?" Casper asked, wrapping her in his arms.

She pushed her face into his neck, drawing in a long sigh of relief. She smelled like dirt, sweat and fear and it made the fury inside him grow. The men she worked with and had grown to trust over the years had done everything in their power to break her spirit.

Every shred of him hated Dragger and John.

"I'm here. I'm going to get us out of this. Whatever you do, just play along," he whispered.

She leaned back and blinked a few times, unaccustomed to the bright light, and gave him a tiny, almost imperceptible nod.

"Where's Travis?" she asked, her voice hoarse.

"He's here?" Casper looked around for her ex, but he was nowhere in sight.

"He came up with me, but his horse threw him. I think he's hurt somewhere, but you need to watch out. He's a part of whatever *this* is." She nodded toward Dragger.

If he was hurt, he had to be here…unless there were other people who had been here to help carry him out. Casper shrugged off the idea. If the men had come up here with the intention of ridding themselves of Lex in order to appease the MC, they would have wanted as few witnesses as possible.

Casper ran his fingers gently over the bump on Lex's right temple where blood had seeped from a small cut and dried on the side of her face. "You're a real bastard, Dragger."

Dragger gave a dismissive laugh. "If you take the deal, we don't have to be death dealers anymore— I'm sure we could convince the MC to continue using our services if we had a CBP agent on our side. We could simply focus on the future. Together, we all could stand to make millions."

Lex tightened in his arms.

"Just think about it, Lawrence, you get everything you want—you'd be set for life and Lex…" Dragger looked to the woman in Casper's arms. "Well, Lex, you can just go back to your job. How 'bout it? I've always liked you. It tore me up thinking about what had to be done up here."

"It couldn't have been too bad for you," Lex spat.

"I know it's hard, but play along, Lex," Casper whispered into her ear. "We have to make it out of here, and our backup is still a ways away."

She looked up at him and closed her eyes, as if she hated what he asked of her.

"So, what exactly do you want Casper to do?" Lex pulled herself out of Casper's arms and winced as she moved. Her fingers moved to her inflamed wrists.

Dragger must have seen the damage, as well. "Damn it, John… I told you no rope. You were supposed to use zip ties. Now look at her."

John answered with a flippant shrug.

"Go get the first-aid kit out of the chalet and check on Travis."

John kicked the dirt as he walked away from them, clearly upset that he didn't get to be privy to their business dealings.

"I'm sorry, Lex. Sincerely. I didn't want you to get hurt," Dragger said, turning back to them. "As I'm sure you are more than aware, Travis and John can both be a little oblivious sometimes."

Oblivious wouldn't have been the word he would have picked for those two scumbags. If he had his way, they'd both be sitting in a federal prison by the end of the year.

Lex snorted a laugh. "We can agree on that. Honestly, I can understand why you picked them as your guys, but what exactly were they doing for you? I mean, what is it that you want Casper and me to start doing?"

"Each week we meet someone on just our side of the border. It used to be the Mounties, who were helping the Keepers north of the border, but they were starting to draw scrutiny. So the last few months we've been working directly with the MC. They hike up from the Waterton side, skirting your border crossing," he said, motioning toward Lawrence.

A sense of impotence filled him. He'd been demoted from FBI to CBP and he couldn't even do that right—at least now he had the chance to rectify the problem.

"I had one of the rangers meet up with one of the bikers. They'd hand off the drugs, and then we'd bring them the rest of the way through the park. We couldn't get caught. We don't run the trade, we're only middlemen."

"So we're basically drug mules."

Dragger laughed. "Nothing as lowly as that. Think about it. We implement the laws here in the park. No one can stop us. Except for this little screw-up— thanks to your ex-husband and his trigger-happy finger—we're above the law. He should have just let the bear have the man. We could have avoided all of this"

"Why did Travis shoot him?" Casper asked.

Dragger shook his head. "No matter what Lex has told you, Travis isn't a bad man… A little private maybe, but in our business that's an asset. When the bear attacked, Travis decided to put

Razor out of his misery instead of letting the beast eat him alive. It was an act of honor and pity."

The word *honor* fit Travis about as well as a cheap suit.

There was the sound of glass breaking and the crack of a gunshot. The men around them hit the deck, dropping down into the dirt, but out of pure instinct, Casper grabbed Lex and sprinted to his place behind the rock, setting her on the ground.

Casper turned. On the other side of the clearing, taking cover behind a tree in the dense stand of the timber, was Steel. Beside him was the pilot.

"Stay here. Don't poke your head up," Casper said to Lex.

"What's going on?" she asked, hugging her knees to her chest.

"Our backup just arrived." He leaned in and took her lips, more than aware that this could be their last kiss.

She let go of her knees and cupped his face, brushing her fingers over his skin.

There was another buzz and crack of a bullet as it cut through the air and struck the rocky side of the chalet. He hesitated but forced himself to break their kiss.

"Lex…" He sighed. "In case something happens, and this all goes to hell in a handbasket, I want you to know I love you."

She pushed a piece of his hair behind his ear. "I love you, too…and I miss your hat."

He hadn't even thought of his hat. He must have left it in the helicopter.

He stood up just in time to hear the crack of the bullet and watch as it ripped through Dragger's chest. He staggered back a few steps and reached up to the hole in his shirt as if in shock.

Blood seeped from the wound above where his heart rested. The gun dropped from his other hand and landed in the dirt. He collapsed beside it.

Even though he was some distance away, Casper could hear the rattle in the man's throat as he drew his last corrupt breath.

Steel and the pilot rushed over. "Are you guys okay?" Steel asked, nearly breathless.

"We're fine. You guys stay here with Lex, make sure she's safe. Travis and John are inside," Casper said.

"Be careful in there. They had to have heard the shooting. They might have laid a trap," Steel said, lifting his chin in the direction of the chalet.

Casper leaned down and gave Lex a kiss, hoping it wouldn't be their last. She gazed up at him; the look in her eyes was that of a woman pleading for him to stay, to keep out of danger, but he couldn't. He had to finish what they started and bring down the other men who were responsible for this mess.

"I'll be back. Everything'll be fine." He turned away before she could ask him to stay. It was hard enough to leave her without hearing her speak those words.

He made his way to the chalet, running from tree to tree, making sure he had cover in case he came under fire. He ran up the steps and stopped beside the door, pressing his body against the cold rock beside it. "John. Travis. Come out with your hands up!" he ordered.

There was nothing. No movement. No sound.

They had to be inside. They couldn't have gone anywhere, not with Travis hurt.

It was now or never.

He stepped in front of the door and, with one swift motion, he kicked it in. The front room was dark. There was an empty table at its center, and Casper made quick work of clearing the room. A hallway ran down the length of the building toward a staircase, and on each side of the shiplapped hall were doors to the guest rooms.

He slipped down the hall. The first guest room was empty. As he moved to the second room, he heard the sound of footsteps inside.

"I know you're in there," he said, moving his body against the wall, careful to keep a bit of distance between himself and the door in case John decided to come out firing. "Come out now. This doesn't have to turn ugly. Just come out with your hands up, and we can do this the easy way."

"There is no easy way—unless you die," John answered.

The door to the room opened, and John lifted his gun. Casper turned toward him. John's eyes were wide with fear and his finger trembled on the trigger.

"Don't do it, John." Casper lifted his gun and pointed it square at the man's chest.

John opened his mouth to speak, but instead his finger squeezed.

Casper dodged, just as the deafening roar of the gun permeated the narrow hall. He fired back. The gun recoiled in his hands, but he kept its aim squarely on John's chest. John stepped back in shock. He slumped against the wall. He closed his eyes as blood seeped from the hole in his chest, and as death took hold, his body slid to the floor with a thump.

John's eyes were open with the unseeing gaze of the dead.

"Travis?" Casper yelled. "Come out, Travis! You're the only one left. There's no other choice. Come along willingly."

"If you want me, you'll have to come get me,"

Travis answered from another of the chalet's rooms near the staircase.

Casper made his way toward the man's voice. "Just come out of the room, Travis. Make this easy on both of us."

Don't make me kill you…

He couldn't bear the thought of what Lex would think if he killed her ex-husband. She might forgive him…or she might resent him for the rest of her life. Yet this man had hurt the woman he loved. Travis had intended on murdering her.

Rage filled him.

Casper had promised that he would never kill in cold blood again, but maybe Travis deserved to die.

The door leading to Travis's room was slightly ajar. Travis sat on the bed, his leg elevated on a pillow and his left arm wrapped in a towel that acted as a sling. On the bed, beside his battered body, was a small-caliber handgun. It looked like a .22. For a moment Casper wondered if it was the same gun that had killed Razor.

Casper aimed his gun at Travis's head as he pushed open the door the rest of the way and walked into the room.

Travis's hand moved toward the gun.

"Unless you want me to shoot, don't touch that gun," Casper said, his finger twitching on the trigger. "Don't give me any more of a reason to shoot your stupid ass."

Travis stopped moving, but his fingers were nearly grazing the black steel of the gun. "We both know that regardless of what I do, you're probably going to shoot me. I saw it splashed all over the internet about how you got kicked out of the FBI."

"You don't know me…"

"No, but I do know what kind of man you are. You're the kind of man who thinks he's above the law."

"I'm not above the law. But I'm going to do what I think is right," Casper argued.

"You keep telling yourself that. You killed a man who wronged you. I've wronged you. We both know you're going to pull that trigger. Your ego won't let you act any other way."

Travis wasn't wrong. He wanted to pull the trigger. He wanted the man to pay for what he'd done and the hurt he'd inflicted on Lex.

"You're a bastard. You'll always be a bastard," Travis said, egging him on. "You don't have self-control when it comes to women."

He pulled the trigger, lifting the barrel of the gun as he shot.

The bullet ripped through the wooden shiplap inches above Travis's head.

Casper's hand shook with anger. "If I didn't

have control, Travis, you'd be dead… As it is, you're going to prison and I'm going to spend the rest of my life with Lex."

Chapter Seventeen

A month had come and gone, and Glacier National Park was buttoned up and ready for the winter—thanks to Lex's efforts as the new head ranger. Snow had started to fall and covered the mountains' tips in white. The cold air bit at her nose as she hiked the highline trail, but after Travis's trial and the events that had unfolded upon his arrival at prison, it felt good to be in nature and away from the stress that had followed them.

Casper was panting behind her.

"Are you okay?" she asked, stopping. "If you want, I can slow down." She gave him a playful smile.

"You're not going to beat me to the top," he said between heaving breaths.

Near the trail was a flat area. It was covered in scree, and between the bits of broken rock were a smattering of late-summer flowers, struggling to flourish in the chill of the fall.

He pointed toward the spot. "Why don't we take a break?" He dropped his backpack and took out the picnic blanket and the lunch they had brought along.

She helped him set out two turkey sandwiches, grapes and a bottle of red wine. As they hiked, she hadn't noticed exactly how beautiful the world was around them. At their feet, the mountain dropped steeply into a valley. In the distance were the remainders of an ancient glacier and the fields of green that were fed by its runoff.

He poured the wine into little plastic cups. "Thank you," she said, taking a sip of the sweet red blend.

"Lex, are you happy?"

The question caught her off guard. "The last few months have been hard, but…" She set down her glass. "Having you at my side has meant everything. Especially after what happened to Travis."

"I'm sorry he's disappeared, Lex… Maybe the bikers had had a hand in it. Maybe they wanted payback for his screw-ups? Who knows. He could have been in deeper than we knew."

"I know. I just don't like the thought of him being out there somewhere. He has to be so angry—if he's alive."

"Don't worry, Steel will get to the bottom of his disappearance." Casper reached over. His hands were hot from their hike as he laced his fingers through hers. "Whatever happens, you need to know that none of this was your fault and I'm going to keep you safe."

"I can't believe I was so blind. I had no idea that he was…what he was. I just thought he was quiet. I didn't know he was a criminal."

"It's not your fault. He was good at what he did—what he *does*."

He picked up a grape and lifted it for her to bite.

It squished, spreading its sweet juice through her mouth as she chewed.

"I'm not perfect, Lex," he said. "And over the last few months, more than anything, I've learned that we gotta take life with both hands." He smiled that half-lipped sexy smile of his and it melted her. "From the first moment I met you, Lex, I've only wanted you…as my wife. Forever."

He reached into the pocket of his jacket and pulled out a gray box. The hinges squeaked as he opened the lid. Inside was a white gold band encrusted with diamonds. Classic and beautiful in all the right ways.

She drew in a breath.

"I hope you like it. I wanted something that you'd love." He took it out and let the box drop to the ground. "Alexis Finch, will you… Will you be my wife?" He moved to his knee as though remembering the formality at the last moment.

The voice in her head that normally told her not to trust, to run away, to expect the worst—it remained silent; and in that moment of freedom, she gave her heart to the man who had taught her how to trust in love.

"Yes, Casper. Yes. I'll marry you."

He slipped the ring on her finger.

She lifted it and the diamonds reflected the world around them. "It's beautiful," she whispered.

"It's just like you. Strong. Bold. Perfect."

"I'm not perfect, Casper," she said with a soft smile.

"To me, you are."

He pulled her into his arms. Together they would have forever, forever to learn and grow, and forever to love.

* * * * *

COMING NEXT MONTH FROM

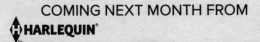
HARLEQUIN®

INTRIGUE

Available February 21, 2017

#1695 HOLDEN
The Lawmen of Silver Creek Ranch • by Delores Fossen
Marshal Holden Ryland needs answers when his ex-flame, Nicky Hart,
steals files from the Conceptions Fertility Clinic—but he never expected
to uncover a black-market baby ring or risk it all for Nicky and her stolen
nephew.

#1696 HOT TARGET
Ballistic Cowboys • by Elle James
Delta Force warrior Max "Caveman" Decker, on loan to Homeland
Security, falls victim to desire on assignment protecting Grace Saunders,
a sexy naturalist who witnessed a murder in backcountry Wyoming.

#1697 ABDUCTION
Killer Instinct • by Cynthia Eden
FBI Special Agent Jillian West returns home to the Florida coast after
working too many tragic cases, but her former lover, navy SEAL
Hayden Black, isn't the only man awaiting her return...

#1698 THE MISSING McCULLEN
The Heroes of Horseshoe Creek • by Rita Herron
Cash Koker has always been a loner out of luck, and when he's accused
of murder, he has no one to turn to except BJ Alexander, a sexy lawyer
ready to put everything on the line to prove her client's innocence.

#1699 FUGITIVE BRIDE
Campbell Cove Academy • by Paula Graves
Security experts Owen Stiles and Tara Bentley are best friends, but their
race for survival against terrorists forces them to confront the true depth
of their relationship—the passion simmering just below the surface.

#1700 SECRET STALKER
Tennessee SWAT • by Lena Diaz
Former lovers SWAT detective Max Remington and Bexley Kane have
a deeply unresolved history between them, but when they're taken
captive by gunmen, addressing the past is the only way for them to find
a future together.

**YOU CAN FIND MORE INFORMATION ON UPCOMING HARLEQUIN® TITLES,
FREE EXCERPTS AND MORE AT WWW.HARLEQUIN.COM.**

HICNM0217

SPECIAL EXCERPT FROM

MIRA®

Join FBI agent Craig Frasier and criminal psychologist Kieran Finnegan as they track down a madman who is obsessed with perfect beauty.

"Horrible! Oh, God, horrible—tragic!" John Shaw said, shaking his head with a dazed look as he sat on his bar stool at Finnegan's Pub.

Kieran nodded sympathetically. Construction crews had found old graves when they were working on the foundations at the hot new downtown venue Le Club Vampyre.

Anthropologists had found the new body among the old graves the next day.

It wasn't just *any* body.

It was the body of supermodel Jeannette Gilbert.

Finding the old graves wasn't much of a shock—not in New York City, and not in a building that was close to two centuries old. The structure that housed Le Club Vampyre was a deconsecrated Episcopal church. The church's congregation had moved to a facility it had purchased from the Catholic church—whose congregation was now in a sparkling new basilica over on Park Avenue. While many had bemoaned the fact that such a venerable old institution had been turned into an establishment for those into sex, drugs and rock and roll, life—and business—went on.

And with life going on…

Well, work on the building's foundations went on, too. It was while investigators were still being called in following the discovery of the newly deceased body— moments before it hit the news—that Kieran Finnegan learned about it, and that was because she was helping out at her family's establishment, Finnegan's on Broadway. Like the old church/nightclub behind it, Finnegan's dated back to just before the Civil War, and had been a pub for most of those years. Since it was geographically the closest place to the church with liquor, it had apparently seemed the right spot at that moment for Professor John Shaw.

A serial killer is striking a little too close to home in the second novel in the **NEW YORK CONFIDENTIAL** *series,* **A PERFECT OBSESSION** *coming soon from* New York Times *bestselling author Heather Graham and MIRA Books.*

$2.⁰⁰ OFF

New York Times **bestselling author HEATHER GRAHAM** brings *perfect* suspense in... **A PERFECT OBSESSION**

Available March 28, 2017

Order your copy today!

MIRA®

$26.99 U.S. / $29.99 CAN.

$2.⁰⁰ OFF

the purchase price of **A PERFECT OBSESSION** by Heather Graham.

Offer valid from March 18, 2017, to September 18, 2017.
Redeemable at participating retail outlets, in-store only. Not redeemable at
Barnes & Noble. Limit one coupon per purchase. Valid in the U.S.A. and Canada only.

52614415

5 65373 00082 3   (8100)0 12232

® and ™ are trademarks owned and used by the trademark owner and/or its licensee.

© 2017 Harlequin Enterprises Limited

MCOUPHG0217

REQUEST YOUR FREE BOOKS!
2 FREE NOVELS PLUS 2 FREE GIFTS!

⬢ HARLEQUIN®

I N T R i G U E

BREATHTAKING ROMANTIC SUSPENSE

YES! Please send me 2 FREE Harlequin® Intrigue novels and my 2 FREE gifts (gifts are worth about $10). After receiving them, if I don't wish to receive any more books, I can return the shipping statement marked "cancel." If I don't cancel, I will receive 6 brand-new novels every month and be billed just $4.74 per book in the U.S. or $5.49 per book in Canada. That's a savings of at least 12% off the cover price! It's quite a bargain! Shipping and handling is just 50¢ per book in the U.S. and 75¢ per book in Canada.* I understand that accepting the 2 free books and gifts places me under no obligation to buy anything. I can always return a shipment and cancel at any time. Even if I never buy another book, the two free books and gifts are mine to keep forever.

182/382 HDN GH3D

Name	(PLEASE PRINT)	
Address		Apt. #
City	State/Prov.	Zip/Postal Code

Signature (if under 18, a parent or guardian must sign)

Mail to the **Reader Service:**
IN U.S.A.: P.O. Box 1867, Buffalo, NY 14240-1867
IN CANADA: P.O. Box 609, Fort Erie, Ontario L2A 5X3
**Are you a subscriber to Harlequin® Intrigue books
and want to receive the larger-print edition?
Call 1-800-873-8635 or visit www.ReaderService.com.**

* Terms and prices subject to change without notice. Prices do not include applicable taxes. Sales tax applicable in N.Y. Canadian residents will be charged applicable taxes. Offer not valid in Quebec. This offer is limited to one order per household. Not valid for current subscribers to Harlequin Intrigue books. All orders subject to credit approval. Credit or debit balances in a customer's account(s) may be offset by any other outstanding balance owed by or to the customer. Please allow 4 to 6 weeks for delivery. Offer available while quantities last.

Your Privacy—The Reader Service is committed to protecting your privacy. Our Privacy Policy is available online at www.ReaderService.com or upon request from the Reader Service.

We make a portion of our mailing list available to reputable third parties that offer products we believe may interest you. If you prefer that we not exchange your name with third parties, or if you wish to clarify or modify your communication preferences, please visit us at www.ReaderService.com/consumerschoice or write to us at Reader Service Preference Service, P.O. Box 9062, Buffalo, NY 14240-9062. Include your complete name and address.

THE WORLD IS BETTER WITH

Romance

Harlequin has everything from contemporary, passionate and heartwarming to suspenseful and inspirational stories.

Whatever your mood, we have a romance just for you!

Connect with us to find your next great read, special offers and more.

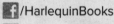

 /HarlequinBooks

 @HarlequinBooks

www.HarlequinBlog.com

www.Harlequin.com/Newsletters

HARLEQUIN®

A *Romance* FOR EVERY MOOD™

www.Harlequin.com